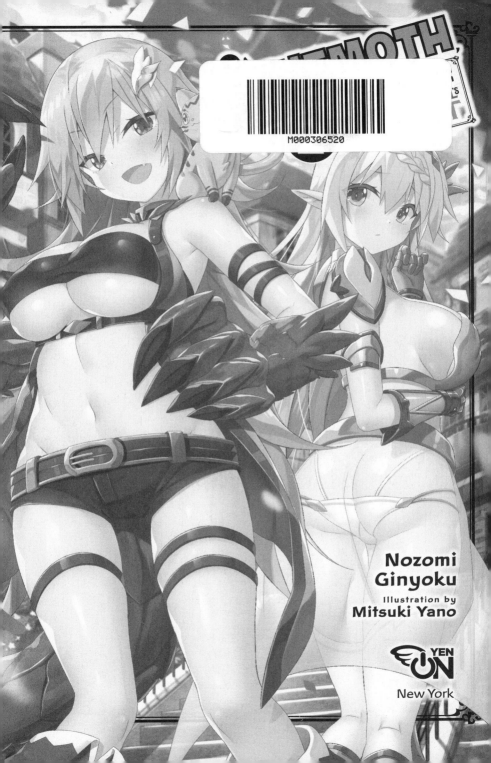

Nozomi
Ginyoku

Illustration by
Mitsuki Yano

YEN
ON

New York

I'm a Behemoth, an S-Ranked Monster, but Mistaken for a Cat,
I Live as an Elf Girl's Pet, Vol. 2
Nozomi Ginyoku

Translation by Caleb DeMarais
Cover art by Mitsuki Yano

S RANKU MONSTAA NO BEHIIMOSU DAKEDO, NEKO TO MACHIGAWARETE ERUFU MUSUME NO PETTO TOSHITE KURASHITEMASU volume 2
©Ginyoku Nozomi ©Yano Mitsuki ©MICRO MAGAZINE, INC.
All rights reserved.
First published in Japan in 2018 by MICRO MAGAZINE, INC.
English translation rights arranged with MICRO MAGAZINE, INC.
through Tuttle-Mori Agency, Inc., Tokyo.

English translation © 2020 by Yen Press, LLC

Yen On
150 West 30th Street, 19th Floor
New York, NY 10001

Visit us at yenpress.com
facebook.com/yenpress
twitter.com/yenpress
yenpress.tumblr.com
instagram.com/yenpress

First Yen On Edition: November 2020

Yen On is an imprint of Yen Press, LLC.
The Yen On name and logo are trademarks of Yen Press, LLC.

The publisher is not responsible for websites (or their content) that are not owned by the publisher.

Library of Congress Cataloging-in-Publication Data
Names: Ginyoku, Nozomi, author. | Yano, Mitsuki, illustrator. | DeMarais, Caleb, translator.
Title: I'm a behemoth, an S-ranked monster, but mistaken for a cat, I live as an elf girl's pet / Nozomi Ginyoku ; illustration by Mitsuki Yano ; translation by Caleb DeMarais.
Other titles: S-rank monster no behemoth dakedo, neko to machigawarete elf musume no pet toshite kurashitemasu. English | I am a behemoth, an S-ranked monster, but mistaken for a cat, I live as an elf girl's pet
Description: First Yen On edition. | New York, NY : Yen On, 2020–
Identifiers: LCCN 2020018429 | ISBN 9781975332945 (v. 1 ; trade paperback) | ISBN 9781975308407 (v. 2 ; trade paperback)
Subjects: CYAC: Fantasy. | Reincarnation—Fiction. | Monsters—Fiction. | Elves—Fiction. | Humorous stories.
Classification: LCC PZ7.1.N698 Sr 2020 | DDC [Fic]—dc23
LC record available at https://lccn.loc.gov/2020018429

ISBNs: 978-1-9753-0840-7 (paperback)
978-1-9753-0841-4 (ebook)

1 3 5 7 9 10 8 6 4 2

LSC-C

Printed in the United States of America

I'M A
BEHEMOTH
an S-Ranked
MONSTER, but MISTAKEN for a CAT,
I Live
as an
2
ELF GIRL'S
PET

Aria

A well-endowed elf girl adventurer. Tama's master.

Tama

A human man and former knight who has been reincarnated as a behemoth. Adopted by Aria.

Stella

A dragon girl who suddenly appears out of nowhere. Lost a battle to Tama and wants to mate with him.

Vulcan

A girl from the tiger-eared clan who runs an item shop. In a party with Aria.

"Tama, come here to my bosom!"

"Meowr—?!" Eep?!

"Tama loves my breasts!"

Tama cries out in fear as Aria and Stella squeeze him between their massive mammaries.

CONTENTS

I am strong. Rather, more accurately, I *once* was strong.

I was born in the darkness. At that time, my body wasn't massive like it is now, but it was still tenacious and rugged. Even as a newborn, I already possessed a certain level of intelligence.

I didn't learn it from anyone, but I know this dark place is called a labyrinth and that I am a monster.

As a newborn, I was attacked by many different monsters: little green slimes, poison-fanged snakes, magic-wielding minotaurs, and small wyverns. But they are all fools. They don't know my strength.

Smaller monsters fall to a single blow from my claws. Midsize monsters are pierced in their weak spots by my tenacious fangs.

Everything was more enjoyable when I was an infant. New monsters attacked me every single day. With each foe I defeated, my body quivered with glee.

That's right—even as a newborn, I took a great deal of pleasure in battle. Before long, I began prowling around the labyrinth in search of greater foes.

The giant iron beast I found had some real bite to it. It was unfazed by my claws and didn't fall to my fangs. But that was all. Even the giant couldn't damage me.

From my perspective, it was nothing more than a massive doll with high defense. Once I realized as much, it went down in just a few blows.

Speaking of challenging foes, human beings are quite the interesting breed. They call themselves adventurers...

They are a race more intelligent than monsters and even on par—no, far beyond myself.

They're weak when alone, but they use shields, swords, magic, and traps as they try to toy with me.

However, they're just as foolish.

If they possess intelligence, they should simply run away. Instead, they see me and yell in excited voices, "It's a dragon! If we take it down, we'll be rich!" and "Our rank and reputation will be unmatched!" before letting loose a number of cunning tricks and attacking me.

I don't know what *"rich"* and *"rank"* mean, but I do know the meaning of the word *"reputation."*

I couldn't hold back a scornful chuckle, thinking of them attacking me with fire in their eyes, not knowing of my strength.

Yet, in the end, I didn't care about their reasons—I was simply eager for the chance to fight.

The humans' swords were incapable of damaging my skin. Their magic was also useless against me—too crude to even have the slightest effect.

"Mid-level magic doesn't work?!"

"My sword technique is worthless?!"

The humans—the adventurers—all cried out in shock as their eyes bulged from their sockets. It seemed these sacks of flesh sorely misjudged their own abilities.

They attacked me with every trick in their book, but in the end, my claws and fangs were their demise. It was the most interesting hunt I'd had in ages.

But nothing more. I've fought a number of human beings since then, but not a single one was able to land a scratch on me.

Until that day.

Before long, I found myself dwelling in the deep reaches of the labyrinth, wallowing in idleness. I realized that no one could match me, and battle had become nothing but troublesome.

Then one day.

Thud—

I felt something fluffy fall on my head.

I have extremely sharpened senses—I soon discerned that a small monster had landed on my head. The tiny monster was looking back and forth, puzzled.

It didn't seem to understand the situation into which it had gotten itself.

"Just how long do you plan to linger on top of me, vulnerable weakling?"

My voice was soft yet rife with anger.

A lower-level monster perching atop my head—the head of a fearsome, strong being—was completely unforgivable.

The tiny monster fell from its place on my head just as I spoke.

It was an orange tabby cat. Or rather, a monster covered in orange tabby fur.

It looked young—likely still a newborn? Even so, it landed on the ground with perfect balance.

However, it looked terrified. It must have finally realized its predicament. Nonetheless, my anger did not subside, despite the tiny monster's appearance.

"You have disturbed my slumber...an offense punishable by death—!!"

I swiped my massive front legs down toward the frightened creature.

"Meown!"

As it cried out, the tiny monster—let's call it the "weakling"—attempted to avoid my attack. Yet, my body is not only gigantic, it's quick. The weakling's evasion was not fast enough. It cried out again.

This time, its body turned to a dull gray. In the next moment—

I heard a shrill, piercing sound. This noise, combined with the resistance I felt, indicated the weakling had activated a skill that hardened its body.

It was unable to completely block my attack, though—my claws dug deeply into the weakling's flesh.

"Grrrawww...you've taken a blow from my claws and survived. I must compliment you...but this is the end."

I paid my respects to the weakling, because even as a cub, it had taken my attack and survived.

But that was the end.

I opened my maw and brought my face close to the weakling. It looked quite delicious—I thought I'd devour it.

However, that was when I made a huge mistake.

"Gwahhhahaaaahahhhh?!"

I let out a shriek.

A sensation unlike any I'd ever felt before was assaulting one of my eyes. In that moment, I realized I was feeling pain for the first time.

Looking out with my still unharmed eye, I perceived a flow of mana and understood.

The source of my pain was a clear, bladelike element extending from the weakling's tail.

Drip...drop...

Blood was falling from my eye and dripping on the ground.

I had been injured by this pitiful creature... Realizing sent my rage soaring to its apex.

I devoted myself to killing it, no matter what! The second I did—

Whoosh—!

A pair of wings sprouted from the weakling's back, and the intruder flew up toward a massive opening in the ceiling.

You dare escape me?!

Even tormented by severe pain, I brought my claws down toward the weakling. Yet—my blow whiffed through thin air. Without one of my eyes, my aim was off.

"Youuuuuuuuuu—gwaaaaaaarrrhhhh!!"

My bloodcurdling invective was earth-shaking.

I do not have wings. For that reason, I was unable to chase after my assailant.

In that moment, I made a promise—if I ever came face-to-face with it again, I would end the weakling's life.

The opportunity came quicker than I expected.

Whoosh—!

After some time had passed, the weakling came to visit me again, accompanied by the sound of its wings.

"Just what do you think you're doing, feeble one? Even though you successfully escaped me once, you now dance back—and for what?"

"Meow!"

The weakling gave a short cry before unleashing a hot breath of flame in my direction.

"Bwa-ha-ha-ha!! What fun!! I will take you on again, yes. And as far as what you did to my eye—I will make you wish you were never born!"

I quivered with great joy as I laughed in the fool's face.

If I can get revenge on the weakling for robbing me of my eye, then I don't care why it returned.

Our battle raged, and I truly wondered if it would continue forever without end. My body became increasingly riddled with small wounds, and conversely, the weakling—no, we'll now call it "small fry"—was completely unscathed.

The small fry had many different skills and, through superior defensive maneuvers, managed to avoid my attacks or completely derail them. It seemed that from our first battle, it'd completely seen through my set of moves.

This was no average small fry. I could no longer call it a weakling.

What a sheer delight it was—the most furious, raging battle I'd ever experienced!

I realized something. I must have been born for this fight. Before long, though, there was a shift in our confrontation.

"Huff...phew..."

The small fry's breathing became ragged. No matter what skills or defensive maneuvers it had, its weakness was being a cub. It was out of stamina.

"Just give up. You cannot defeat me. Give in to death," I told it.

I planned to obliterate the small fry without hesitation. It would be a form of respect for this puny creature who had managed to survive this long in battle with me.

But what is the meaning of this?

The small fry showed no sign of giving up. If anything, its expression conveyed sheer conviction.

It was in the next moment that it happened.

Flash—!!

The small fry's body erupted in a flash of light. When the brilliance receded, a massive lacquer-black feline beast was revealed.

"*Wrrroooarrrhhh!!!*"

The beast roared, and my body shook from the deafening noise.

What nonsense! There is no way I am afraid, I thought.

Then the beast spoke.

"My name is Tama—!! I am the knight of the adventurer Aria and an S-ranked monster, behemoth! In order to save my master's life, I will be taking yours!!"

Its voice had changed along with its appearance. Yet, hearing its name, I sensed something. The lacquer-black beast in front of me was the same small fry I'd been fighting the entire time.

The rest was a one-way street. The small fry...no—the "Fearsome Cat"—expelled a hellfire from its maw that easily scorched my skin. I felt my life in danger and, for the first time ever, attempted to escape.

But—

"Bwohhh—!!"

Rushing through the flames, the Fearsome Cat leaped and landed directly in front of me as I attempted to withdraw. A massive blade of flame was extending from the tip of its tail, and it was already heading straight for me.

I can't get away!

That much I knew. By this point, we were about to clash.

I brought my front claws across in a sideswipe. However, as it brought down its flaming tail, the Fearsome Cat twisted its body to the side in a maneuver to prevent any fatal damage.

As for me...

Slash—!!

With the accompanying sound, I felt my face being sliced open from the side.

This is defeat...absolute, certain defeat...

Before I actually felt any pain, my heart grew heavy with this fact.

And I thought...if I was ever to be "reborn," I would want to mate with a being of this Fearsome Cat's caliber and produce offspring...

With that, my consciousness plunged into darkness.

It's morning. In a room of an inn tucked away in Labyrinthos, a beast—a small orange tabby—awakens on the bed to the sound of birds chirping. Its adorable golden eyes are still narrowed, sleepy.

Its name is Tama.

It's a rare creature—an elemental cat—which is a feline species... At least, that's what its master thinks. In reality, the beast is a calamity-level S-ranked monster, a behemoth—albeit still a cub. In addition, this is its reincarnated form, and it still has all its memories from its previous life.

The behemoth is a male.

In his previous life, he was an honorable knight, and he'd protected humans from demons and monsters on innumerable occasions through his masterful swordsmanship.

Now, however, Tama's entire body is enveloped in a warm, squishy embrace.

"You're awake, Tama! Hee-hee, you're so cute today, as always."

Just as Tama feels swathed by this comforting snugness, he hears a voice ring out above him. It belongs to Aria—his master and the source of the doting hug.

She has porcelain-white skin and platinum-blond hair down to her waist. Her eyes are cool…but their ice-blue tone also imparts a sense of affection. As an elf girl, Aria's beauty is unrivaled.

Not to mention, her breasts are so ripe and heavy that you wouldn't believe it. Their bounty is only comparable to "melon class."

"Meowwwr!"

Tama mews lovingly as Aria smiles at him and rubs his face on her breasts, fawning on her.

In his previous life, Tama was a full-grown knight, and he still has his memories from back then. Now, though, he's a cub. His young body tugs at the heartstrings, and Aria can't help but dote on him.

"Ohhh… Tama, you are such a little lover boy…!"

When Tama nuzzles her, Aria's voice turns sweet and coquettish, and her eyes light up.

Aria loves Tama.

She loves him in the sense that one can feel love for a small animal…but there is another aspect to her feelings, too. She is *in love* with him. Aria is, by nature— Rather, she has somewhat unconventional proclivities.

Basically, Aria sees the cub Tama, a different species, as both her pet and a member of the opposite sex.

Yikes… I did it again. I can't help but rub up on her.

Realizing that Aria's breathing has become rough and excited, Tama quickly comes back to his senses and quickly moves away from her.

Tama knows that if he's overly affectionate with Aria, her switch—known as her erotic switch—will get flipped, and she'll start speeding down a certain path.

"Ohhh… But you should love on me even more…"

Aria sounds downright dejected. She puts her index finger in her mouth, looking like she wants something, and rubs her thighs together, now fully exposed between her pure-white negligee.

The scene is utterly captivating, and Tama's behemoth is threatening to go full behemoth. If she sees that, though, it will be over.

There is no denying that Aria will eventually take Tama's chastity. For now, Tama controls himself according to his knight's honor and manages to hold back.

After she finishes twitching, Aria sighs lightly and speaks to Tama.

"Mmmm…phew… Okay, I guess I can hold off, too. Should we get ready to go out?"

"Meow—!!"

Aria begins shuddering ever so slightly, then lets out a small breath before addressing Tama.

That trembling she did just now… Was that…? Tama wonders, but he pretends like he didn't see anything and answers Aria excitedly.

Today, Tama and Aria are planning to go on a picnic in a nearby forest. It's the last day of their rest and relaxation.

Tomorrow, Aria intends to resume her occupation as an adventurer.

Just one month ago, Aria was infected by poison in her battle with a demon and was on the verge of death. Thanks to Tama, she acquired the source of the only antidote—an earth dragon's eye—and managed to survive. Regardless, the poison ravaged her body and greatly damaged her endurance and strength.

She was simply unable to fight in that state. That's why, for the past month, she pledged to devote herself to eating well and regaining her strength.

"Okay—first, I'll change!"

Aria begins taking off her snowy negligee, exposing her bare skin.

Hmm. My master is as gorgeous as ever.

Aria's thin arms and legs—and perfectly tight waist—are porcelain white. Her twin peaks, only describable as melon-size, are constrained by a black bra, and her soft posterior is ensconced in a black thong.

Though Aria is every bit a wholesome elf girl, the design of her underwear is provocative. The stark gap between her personality and this appearance is absolutely bewitching, but before Tama can become fully licentious, he is absolutely dumbstruck by her pure beauty.

Ooh... Tama can't keep his eyes off my body... It makes me throb when he does that...

Aria is getting all hot and bothered yet again by Tama's gaze... but Tama doesn't realize it.

"Okay, now it's time for you to change, too, Tama!"

Aria has outfitted herself in a stark white blouse and a black skirt, both with slight frills—you might call this her "virgin killer" outfit. She turns to Tama and smiles, holding a piece of clothing in her hand.

A few minutes later...

"Ooooh!! Soooo cute!"

"Meow..." *This garb is a disgrace.*

Aria sounds beyond elated, while Tama is clearly not having it.

Tama is now dressed in an article of feline wear—a light-blue fabric with stark white frills. It's a gothic dress for cats.

On the inside, Tama is a proud knight, and here he's being made to sport a cat dress...

For Tama, this is a disgrace.

It's too bad. Tama is absolutely adorable, and paired with his cuteness, the dress couldn't suit him any better.

What's more, Aria paid a hefty price having this piece custommade at a garment shop in Labyrinthos.

When she saw the finished product, her expression was one of true happiness. Seeing this, there was no way that Tama could refuse putting it on for her.

Boing—!

Tama leaps onto Aria's breasts, and she holds him tight, beaming from ear to ear as she leaves the inn.

"Look, I found some blackberries!"

Shortly after arriving at their forest destination, Aria discovers a patch of ripe blackberries.

"What great timing. Let's take some and eat them for dessert after our picnic!"

"Meown—!!"

Hearing the word *picnic*, Tama regains some pep in his step, having been dejected from being made to wear his female cat dress.

Aria collects some blackberries and finds a convenient place to sit down before opening the basket she's brought along. It contains sandwiches the innkeeper made.

"Okay, Tama, open wide!"

"Meow—"

Aria pushes one of the sandwiches toward Tama. He opens his tiny mouth and chomps down on it.

Oh! This is delicious, absolutely delectable.

Tama's golden eyes grow wide.

The sandwiches contain fresh lettuce, smoked chicken, and a special sauce. The taste of the sweet lettuce, umami-rich chicken, and slightly spicy sauce has Tama quite ravenous.

"Hee-hee, that's a good boy. ♪"

Aria smiles lovingly at him and grabs another sandwich in her other hand to take a bite.

As Aria eats, Tama realizes she has sauce on her mouth.

Hmm? Master, you have sauce on the side of your mouth. Tsk...
Boing—!

Tama leaps effortlessly and lands silently on Aria's shoulder.

"What's going on, Tama?"

After he suddenly leaps onto her, Aria looks at Tama quizzically. Tama then leans toward her lips...and licks her with his tiny tongue. In the past month, while Aria has been quite weak, Tama's become a bit overprotective of her.

When she washes her face, he'll bring her a towel, tending to Aria and her needs whenever possible. Just now, he again took care to groom Aria's face.

Aria, realizing that Tama jumped on her to lick the spot on her mouth clean, laughs quietly and says, "That tickles... Thank you. You are so sweet, Tama. I can't thank you enough for saving my life twice—well, at the very least, once..."

When she encountered a goblin mage in the labyrinth, Tama saved her from mortal danger.

She was also thanking him for defeating an earth dragon to collect its eye, the only known antidote for the demon poison that ravaged her body.

Aria said *"at the very least, once..."* because she doesn't have proof that Tama actually did the latter.

No, it is I who cannot thank you enough. If you hadn't saved me when I was injured in the labyrinth, my life would be very different.

Tama is immensely grateful for Aria, because when he had just reincarnated, the earth dragon had dealt him an almost fatal blow, and Aria had saved him.

This is why Tama has pledged his allegiance to Aria and devoted himself as her knight.

"Meown—!!"

"Ooh, Tama, that's so ticklish."

Tama is rubbing his head against Aria's cheek in an expression of thanks.

She complains that it's ticklish, but she looks delighted as she strokes Tama lovingly.

The bond between cat and elf girl has deepened even further today.

Midnight, on the day of the picnic:

"Meown, meown, meown— ♪"

Tama is in high spirits as he takes a solo stroll through Labyrinthos.

When Aria sleeps, she leaves the window in her room open a crack and lets Tama come and go as he pleases. From time to time, Tama slips into the darkness and enjoys a midnight walk.

He's in high spirits due to the satisfying picnic they had that afternoon.

Mm, the city is definitely looking great tonight.

As he trots along, Tama thinks about how exceptionally beautiful Labyrinthos is. At night, the streetlights powered by magic that line the city roads give off an orange glow, lighting up the cobblestone streets, the stone homes, and the water running in the canals. The entire city seems so welcoming.

Even though it's midnight, a number of couples are seated along the canals shoulder to shoulder, taking in the resplendent cityscape.

The streetlights in Labyrinthos were installed by the lords of the city, the Marquis Estate, to ensure public order.

"Oh? Is that you, Tama?"

"Wow, rare to see you at this time of night. Out for a stroll?"

As Tama walks toward the north end of the city, two men in armor and helmets appear. One has close-cropped hair and is wearing light armor, while the other is a lizard man wearing heavy gear.

These are Danny, second in command of the knights' guard, and the knight Howard.

Tama gives a hearty meow in greeting, as if to say *Good evening!* to the pair of men.

"Nothing wrong with a stroll, but don't stay out too long, okay? If you don't remain close to Aria, she'll get sad in a heartbeat."

"That's right. A knight must never cause his master to lament."

Danny stoops low to pet Tama as the officer offers this warning. Howard agrees with the sentiment, taking some portable provisions in the form of jerky from his chest pocket and tearing them into strips before giving a bit to Tama.

Of course. Danny, Howard, I would never, ever cause my master sorrow!

Tama stuffs his cheeks with the jerky from Howard and nods repeatedly in response.

"Heh-heh, from the look of it, there's no problem here."

"Yes. He's a genuinely intelligent cat."

Apparently satisfied with Tama's response, the two men turn in the direction from which Tama came and disappear into the distance.

Tama hears them saying, "Ahhh, finally time to change shifts," and realizes that the pair are on night patrol.

Hmmmm. I got a midnight snack, so maybe I should be on my way, too. I want to get back before my master awakens.

Tama audibly swallows the jerky and sprints off to one location in particular.

The labyrinth—it's been quite some time.

Tama stands in the darkness. Rocky crags spread in every direction from this bone-chilling place...

This is the labyrinth, a den of monsters.

Tama didn't leave home just for a midnight stroll. He's come this far with a specific objective in mind.

Just what is it? Checking his current status will be the quickest way to understand.

Name: Tama
Type: : Behemoth (cub)
Innate Skills: Elemental Howl, Skill Absorb,
Elemental Tail Blade, Divine Lion Protection
Absorbed Skills: Storage, Poison Fang, Flight,
Fireball, Icicle Lance, Iron Body, Summon
Tentacle, Endless Mucus Blast, Crossbreed,
Dragon Fang, Dragon Claw

First, *evolution possible* has disappeared from the bottom of Tama's status. For some unknown reason, since defeating the earth dragon a month earlier, the words have vanished.

Hmm. Evolution isn't appearing on my status today, either... No worries, I have other plans anyway.

There's nothing more reassuring than being able to use Evolution when the going gets rough. Yet, there's no helping the fact it's not here.

Tama is disappointed, but he changes his perspective and focuses his attention elsewhere.

A new innate skill, Divine Lion Protection, and the absorbed skills Dragon Fang and Dragon Claw. I wonder what those are...

Tama ponders as he stares at the skill names. He noticed Divine Lion Protection a few days after defeating the earth dragon. Dragon Fang and Dragon Claw are skills he gained after sneaking out to take a bite of the earth dragon's corpse during the few days Aria spent recovering in Renald.

Okay, let's start by trying out these absorbed skills... Oh, and there's a perfect test subject.

Tama has come to the labyrinth to see the effects of his newly acquired skills. Starting tomorrow, he'll resume adventuring with Aria, so this is his best opportunity to experiment.

Moments earlier, a grotesque figure appeared in front of Tama screeching, "Gugi—!!" It has green skin and is no taller than a child, with short horns protruding from its head like a miniature demon—this is a goblin, an E-ranked monster.

Seeing Tama, the goblin raises its shoddy dagger above its head and screeches harshly, drool streaming from its mouth as it rushes toward him.

Okay, let's start by trying out Dragon Fang. Against a goblin, even if the skill misfires, I'll have time to recover.

His mind made up, Tama unleashes the skill against the goblin charging him.

"Meown!" *Dragon Fang!*

Tama mews adorably as he leaps forward. Judging from its name, he's predicted the skill's effect to an extent and encroaches on the goblin with his tiny mouth open wide.

However, the moment he goes in to bite the goblin's abdomen— something happens.

Psssh—!!

There's a sharp hiss. Looking down, Tama sees a torrent of blood gushing from multiple wounds on the goblin's body. At the same time, the sensation of having bitten down hard on something rushes through Tama's jaw.

Given the state of the goblin in front of him and the way his jaw feels, Tama realizes what has happened.

Dragon Fang…what a terrifying skill! I can't believe it simulates the actual phenomenon *of biting into flesh…*

Tama is astonished. Using the power of mana, the Dragon Fang skill creates a massive, gaping jaw in midair, linked to the movement of his own mouth, allowing him to go in for a powerful bite attack.

This is certainly a skill worthy of being obtained by taking a bite from an S-ranked monster. It's not quite as powerful as Elemental Howl or Elemental Tail Blade, but unlike those, it doesn't require charging up or direct manipulation, making it quite convenient. I will use it accordingly.

An experienced knight, Tama understands the characteristics

of Dragon Fang immediately, deciding exactly when and how he will employ it.

Okay, next up is Dragon Claw... Or it should be, but I think I should test the skill's effect on a midsize monster or larger. I'll delve a bit deeper into the labyrinth.

The little behemoth had originally intended to enter the labyrinth only to test his skills, but seeing that they are much more powerful than he imagined, the knight within him is exhilarated. Compelled by an impetus to take on an even greater foe, Tama ventures farther into the monsters' den.

"Bu-hiiiiiiiii—!"

On the third level of the labyrinth, a monster with a pig face—an orc—appears, accompanied by its moronic squeal. Upon seeing Tama, it launches into its boorish, loud advance.

Okay, time to test out my next skill.

Keeping his eye on the approaching orc, Tama prepares to test his second newly acquired skill. He's already vanquished two orcs using Dragon Fang, both of which went down in a single blow.

The skill gleaned from the S-rank monster is very strong. Now that he understands its power and usability, Tama is ready to test the effects of his next skill.

"Meow—!" *Eat this—Dragon Claw!*

With a miniature roar, he rips down on the encroaching orc with his right front paw.

"Bu-gyaaaaa—!"

The orc's bloodcurdling scream echoes through the labyrinth.

Seeing Dragon Fang's effects, Tama had already assumed how Dragon Claw would work to an extent. And he was right.

Before his front paw actually connects with the orc's body, four thick claw marks rip into the creature, and a massive amount of blood erupts from them.

The sensation of having hit something hard lingers in Tama's paw. The effects of Dragon Claw are similar to Dragon Fang—a gigantic claw is manifested in the air through the power of mana. Linked to the movement of his own arm, it allows him to unleash an attack.

Mm—this skill is supremely useful as well. With this, I can now employ a powerfully balanced five-tiered attack pattern: bite, scratch, howl, tail blade, and magic.

Tama nods emphatically before the orc, which has collapsed in a heap from intense pain and blood loss. The little behemoth licks his front paw and grooms his face.

Okay, time to test out my last new skill, Divine Lion Protection.

Tama has used Dragon Claw to dispatch a number of orcs and ropers with a single blow to each and has now arrived at the fifth level of the labyrinth.

He surveys the area to make sure there aren't any monsters around before activating his innate skill Divine Lion Protection.

Unlike Dragon Fang and Dragon Claw, he has no idea what Divine Lion Protection will entail from its name alone.

Realizing that using the skill when pitted against an actual enemy in the fifth level could be dangerous, Tama has decided to activate his skill now, even though it may not connect with anything.

Here we go! Divine Lion Protection!!

Tama incants the spell in his mind. And then…

Flash—!!

His body is enveloped in a bright golden light, and a hot sensation erupts from deep within his core. Tama then realizes that a number of statuses are being bestowed on his body simultaneously.

The innate skill Divine Lion Protection grants a plethora of superior benefits, among them: increased stamina, increased defense, poison resistance, flame resistance, ice resistance, and shock resistance.

Tama also understands that these effects apply not only to him but to those around him as well.

What a magnificent skill. Activating it before battle will allow me to protect my master in the face of enemies who use poison, like the nefarious Beryl. It is certainly a divine form of protection, just like the name says!

As Aria's pet (knight), having a number of ways to keep her as safe as possible is always welcome.

In reality, the skill Divine Lion Protection appeared after Tama failed to protect Aria. He'd prayed for a means to defend her, and the skill became manifest alongside his evolution.

"Mwooohhh—"

As Tama sits astonished by the power of Divine Lion Protection, a monster appears from the rocky shadows, grunting. It's a demi-human bovine beast—a minotaur.

It's holding a giant ax in one hand and glaring at Tama with blood surging in its eyes. It definitely wants to eat this feline morsel whole.

Maybe I should use Dragon Claw... No, I should see just how powerful the effects of Divine Lion Protection really are.

As the minotaur approaches him, Tama makes up his mind and wiggles his kitty butt back and forth, ready to strike at any moment...

Thwomp!

He then kicks off the ground and flies forward with lightning speed—he's like a bullet as he races toward the minotaur's abdomen and bashes into it headfirst.

"Mwooohhh—?!"

The minotaur cries out in agony and doubles over, clutching its stomach. No surprise, given Tama's velocity. On the other hand, how did Tama fare from the blow?

It...doesn't hurt?

He's standing next to the minotaur, slightly bewildered. He

expected to take the same amount of damage as the minotaur, having blasted full tilt into its rock-hard stomach. To his surprise, however, Tama feels no pain whatsoever.

Initially puzzled by this, he soon recalls the effects of the divine protection bestowed upon him, and his bewilderment ceases.

That's right! Divine Lion Protection also has the effect of greatly enhancing defenses. But I didn't think it would be this much... This is a truly reassuring skill.

Tama is blown away by the powerful effects of Divine Lion Protection, although currently they're benefiting only him. If he uses it in tandem with the defensive skill Iron Body, he'll undoubtedly become covered in rigid, strong defensive armor... His thoughts are filled with the possibilities.

No, no—this is no good. I'm still in the middle of battle. I need to finish this beast off.

Tama returns his attention to the minotaur, crying out in pain, and brings up one of his front paws, mewing loudly. He's activated his absorbed skill Dragon Claw.

A massive gash erupts from the minotaur's head to its abdomen, and fresh blood spews. The minotaur falls silently to the ground.

Now that I've tested out all my new skills, it's about time I return to my master's side.

Tomorrow, Aria will resume her activities as adventurer. If possible, Tama wants to return to her before morning. Just as he was thinking as much—

"I've finally found you, Fearsome Cat!"

Tama hears the words ring in his ears.

"Meown?!" *Who's there?*

Tama whips around and assumes battle position. Looking in the direction of the voice, he finds...a beautiful girl, all alone. Her sharp eyes are golden in color and her long, disheveled hair is flaxen. She's wearing only a single tattered tunic for clothing. The thin fabric barely covers her large breasts and proportionate, thick thighs.

Why the hell is she down here in the labyrinth, looking like that? And did she just call me "Fearsome Cat"? This... I've felt this feeling...somewhere before...

Tama is absolutely bewildered at the girl's sudden appearance. At the same time, he's experiencing powerful déjà vu. Paying him no regard, the girl in the tattered tunic says, "Well, well, Fearsome Cat, I see you've turned back into your younger form. No matter. More importantly..."

At this, the girl suddenly rushes toward Tama, screaming, "Come, Fearsome Cat! You must copulate with meeeeeeeeeeee!!"

"Meowwwwwwn!!" *Oh god, she's a deviant, just like master!*

Tama has no idea who this girl is, but he does know she's totally insane!

Having reached this conclusion, when the girl approaches him, he decides to make a break for it.

"Meown—!" *Phew, looks like I managed to shake her off my tail.*

The second layer of the labyrinth—Tama hides behind a rock outcropping and sighs quietly. His face is worn with intense exhaustion.

As it should be—his cat-and-mouse theater with the girl in the tattered tunic went on for close to an hour. The entire time, she complained, "Why do you run from me, Fearsome Cat?" and "Please! I need your seed!"—a litany of incomprehensible nonsense as she chased after him.

To make matters worse, she was inexplicably fast. Even as a cub, Tama is quite quick, but she continually caught up with him easily.

Realizing that she was definitely close to catching him, Tama switched his escape plan from an all-out dash to a back-and-forth scramble employing feints behind the rock outcroppings. He then traveled a highly dangerous route that directly connects the fifth and second levels of the labyrinth and somehow managed to escape her.

"Where are youuuuuu, Fearsome Cat—?! Copulate with meeeeeee—!!"

Her voice reverberates from the depths of the mazelike tunnels.

Oh shit—if I stay here, she'll find me for sure! I have to get out of here!

Without a chance to properly catch his breath, Tama jogs for the exit.

Somehow, he escapes without the girl spotting him again.

"Meown—!" *Uggghhh, that was terrifying, master...*

Tama has made his way back to Aria's room. After the horrific experience of being chased by a mysterious girl demanding his chastity, he dives right into the middle of Aria's bed without thinking twice.

Although he was a full-grown knight in his previous life, now Tama is just a behemoth cub. He's controlled by the emotions of his young body and soon begins fawning against and cuddling his master, Aria, without a second's hesitation. That comes with the territory of reincarnation.

Squeeze—

A warm, soft sensation accompanied by a sweet fragrance envelops Tama as he dives into the bed.

"Hee-hee... Tama, you're so soft and cuddly—it feels amazing."

Aria's voice. She's still sleepy as she softly embraces the kitten now ensconced in the covers.

Phew... Being between my master's breasts is so soothing...

Although he was tense from his recent terror, now wrapped in Aria's soft warmth and smelling her unique maternal, sweet scent, Tama naturally loosens up.

But really, who was that girl? She was screaming that she wants my seed...and there was something vaguely familiar about her...

Even in between Aria's breasts, the little behemoth can't help but think of the gorgeous mystery girl.

Regardless, Tama is very tired. Before he can solve the mystery, he falls fast asleep in the warmth of Aria's breasts.

"Meown—!! Aria, Tama, good morning—!!"

It's early morning, and in front of Labyrinthos's guild, a girl sees Aria with Tama tucked between her breasts, and she waves at them.

Her bare skin is amber, and she's wearing overalls and an apron. Thanks to her outfit, her cleavage and side boob are in open view, and her cat ears are twitching back and forth atop her head of dark golden hair. She carries a massive battle hammer, nearly as tall as she is, on her back.

Her name is Vulcan, and she's a girl from the tiger-eared clan, the blacksmith in this city, and a member of Aria's adventurer party.

"Good morning, Vulcan!"

"Meowwwr!"

Aria and Tama turn toward her and return her greeting enthusiastically. Vulcan replies with, "Awww, Tama is as cute as always! ♪" before taking him from Aria and tucking him securely in between her amber-colored breasts peeking out from her overalls.

Hers aren't as big as Aria's, but they're still very ripe and juicy. They're smooth and bouncy, with the perfect amount of give. Ensconced against the warmth of Vulcan's bare skin, Tama's eyes narrow in pleasure.

"Hee-hee, Tama looks so blissful... And with his new equipment, he's cute as can be. ♡"

Seeing Tama being held by Vulcan, Aria looks absolutely spellbound.

"Tama's new equipment is supercute, but, Aria, you look amazing in yours, too!" Vulcan assures Aria, who's still writhing in infatuation staring at Tama.

Just as Vulcan said, Aria and Tama both have brand-new

equipment. First, Aria's new ensemble is what's commonly known as "bikini armor." It's the same kind that Keni and Marietta wore when they accompanied her on the previous quest to slay the demon, but Aria's has been crafted to look even more suggestive.

Paired with her overwhelming melons, her current attire will absolutely turn heads. At the same time, the elf is the picture of sheer beauty—not only lust.

Her suit is made from the material orichalcum, a rare metal, combined with steel in an alloy. Orichalcum is more resilient than steel and less weighty, with a light-blue hue. Its price also puts steel to shame, and even combined with steel in an alloy, there's no way an adventurer of Aria's rank could afford it. However, the young woman recently came into a large sum of money.

She received some compensation for defeating the demon Beryl in her last quest…but the largest sum she earned came by way of the trolls that Tama defeated recently. Troll skin, meat, and bones can be sold for an incredibly high price.

The knights who'd accompanied her on the quest had passed the money on to her, insisting that because Tama defeated them, she should take it as his master. Using these funds, Aria had asked Vulcan, her partner, to create brand-new equipment for Tama and herself.

The orichalcum-alloy bikini armor is a translucent shade of silver-blue, matching her porcelain-white skin and platinum-blond hair perfectly, amplifying her beauty even further. Her appearance resembles a Valkyrie from the world of mythology.

Above all, Aria's bikini armor doesn't hinder the effects of her innate skill, Acceleration. That said, her equipment now includes gauntlets and leggings, which her previous outfit did not, allowing for improved defenses as well—truly an incredible piece of craftsmanship. The bikini armor full set includes shoulder flaps, gauntlets, and high leggings, all created from the orichalcum alloy.

Previously, Aria wore gloves and high boots to prevent her movement from being impeded, but thanks to how light orichalcum is, she was able to increase the number of defensive armaments she has equipped.

Brand-new defensive equipment isn't Aria's only new gear. She has new weapons, too.

"This color… There's no way this is also made from orichalcum, is it?"

"Sure is, meow. And it's not your average orichalcum alloy! It's mixed with *tamahagane*! Depending on your skill, you could probably cut through steel like butter!"

Vulcan brings out a certain knife and recommends it to Aria as they converse. The knife's blade is the same silver-blue, but it's an even stronger hue than Aria's defensive armament.

Just like Vulcan said, this knife has the pure-iron sand-based metal *tamahagane* mixed in. *Tamahagane* is said to be the best material for honing the sharpest-possible blade edges.

In fact, if an experienced swordsman wields a weapon created with this metal, it is very possible to cleave through steel with ease. What's more, this particular knife is a *tamahagane*-and-orichalcum alloy. It has the honed edge of *tamahagane* but is lighter than steel—it will not chip or nick under normal circumstances, Vulcan explains.

Next is Tama's equipment. Until recently, he had been wearing a helmet and leather armor, but now that's changed to a silver-blue helm and matching body armor. He looked cute in his former adventurer defensive armament, but this getup, which has him almost looking like he's cosplaying as a knight, is adorable, too.

For Aria, who calls her companion her knight, his current appearance is nearly more than she can bear. Tama is also very fond of his current equipment. As is evident from its color, his new gear is made from an orichalcum alloy, just like Aria's bikini armor.

Since orichalcum is much lighter compared to other metals, Tama actually feels less weighted down than before. With this orichalcum defensive armament, his defensive capacity has increased manifold.

Using Iron Body and his new skill Divine Lion Protection, he is more capable than ever of protecting his master. Armed with these new tools, Tama can now very feasibly take an attack from a dragon and survive.

"Okay, let's head out meow!"

"Okay! Thank you so much, Vulcan."

"Meown—!!"

The two girls and Tama exchange words and mews before heading off toward the labyrinth.

I won't be seeing her again, will I…?

The mystery girl he encountered last night pops into Tama's head as he ponders the possibility. Little does he know that likelihood is greater than he could have imagined…

"The labyrinth… I get nervous when I haven't been here for a while."

"Our instincts are probably dulled because it's been some time since we engaged in combat. Be on your guard!"

Aria steps into the labyrinth and shivers at the sensation of its unique aura on her skin. Vulcan puts her hand on her shoulder and smiles sweetly while advising caution.

Aria and Vulcan are both C-ranked adventurers. Normally, none of the monsters on the first level of the labyrinth would pose a challenge to them, but Aria hasn't fought at all during her month of rehabilitation.

For this reason, their first goal is taking out some low-level monsters like goblins and slimes. Today's objective is for Aria to regain her instincts as an adventurer.

"Meown—!"

"…? What's the matter, Tama?"

Just as Aria and Vulcan make their way to find some easy

pickings, Tama cries out at them. The two women turn around and look at him, puzzled.

However, Aria knows that Tama isn't just crying out without reason. She can understand what he's thinking, to an extent, based on the timbre of his voice and his expression.

My master hasn't fought in some time. Even though Vulcan and I are here, there's no harm in having a little extra insurance. I will activate divine protection before we come across any monsters. Here goes…

"Meown!" *Divine Lion Protection!*

Tama gives another adorable mew in Aria and Vulcan's direction. A soft golden light envelops the bodies of the trio.

"Meow—what's this…?!"

"How incredible! My stamina and defense… All my resistances have been boosted! Tama, is this your power?"

Aria and Vulcan, wrapped in the golden glow of Divine Lion Protection, cry out in surprise. Both have realized that their stats have been buffed across the board.

"Meown—!"

Tama answers Aria with an adorable mew that says, *How you like me now?*

When Tama first met the woman who would become his master, he was scared that she'd realize he isn't an elemental cat but a behemoth, and he used only a select few skills for that reason. However, during her duel with the aristocrat Kussman, he was forced to use his Elemental Howl and, subsequently, was conveniently mistaken as an elemental cat with innate skills. Now, to protect Aria, he can employ a number of abilities without hesitation.

"Meow, Tama, just how many different skills do you have, meow? You're incredible for just a little kitty, meow!"

"The ones he used on Beryl's minions were very powerful, but I did not expect him to have this level of advanced support skills, too. He's activated a buff on our stamina and defense and given us resistance boosts in all categories—I've never even heard of such an effect. That he hasn't used it so far must mean he acquires new skills as he grows up...?!"

Discussing Tama's beyond-normal specs, Vulcan lightly defers to his master, Aria, as the girls converse.

Tama himself can only cock his head to the side, as if to say, *What now?*

Seeing him, Aria and Vulcan can't help but chuckle to themselves dryly.

"Perhaps, but his combat instincts are a huge help, especially since my own battle prowess has dulled a bit. Thank you, Tama! ♡"

"Meown—!"

There's love and gratitude in Aria's voice, and Tama responds enthusiastically.

Vulcan stares at the two of them with a tinge of jealousy in her eyes. In that moment...

"Gu-gi—!"

A grating shriek pierces Tama's ears. A single goblin has appeared a ways down the tunnel.

"A goblin. I'm nervous to be fighting for the first time in a while, but Tama's boost to my power has me feeling better. Let's go...!"

Aria speaks and rushes forward with quick, quiet steps. Just like she said, there is no nervousness in her stride. Why should there be?

The Divine Lion Protection that Tama activated also grants additional resistance to fear. Plus, Aria already has a deep conviction to become a strong, righteous person just like her hero, the Holy Blade.

If someone who expresses such noble aims is released from fear, it's only natural they will act without hesitation.

So fast! Aria hasn't even activated her innate skill, Acceleration, but she's unusually quick.

Of course, she's not as quick as when she's using Acceleration, but she's definitely eclipsed the realm of speed possible for a normal human.

"M-meow?! She's that fast without Acceleration? Must be the effect of Tama's buff... Absolutely incredible, I say again..."

Seeing Aria's speed at work in front of her, Vulcan's eyes go wide in shock.

Slash—!

A single, silver-blue arc gleams through the dimly lit space, followed by a bewildered cry.

"Gu-gya...?"

It's the goblin, and its face looks just as puzzled as the sound of its wail.

Flop...

The creature's head falls to the ground with a *thud*, and soon after, fresh blood gushes from the new hole in its neck. There isn't any light in its eyes as the goblin's head tumbles across the ground.

The monster never even saw what was coming—not the stunningly gorgeous elf girl Aria or the single knife swipe that took its head clean off.

Incredible! What speed, even without activating Acceleration. And the tamahagane-*and-*orichalcum-alloy *blade that Vulcan tempered for her... She was just aiming for its jugular, but the goblin's entire head went flying. Truly amazing...!*

Aria hasn't wielded her knives against a monster in some time. She was worried she wouldn't be able to take it down in a single blow, but seeing how far this battle has exceeded her expectations, she is relieved and excited.

If she adds Acceleration to the mix...she'll be as fast as a bolt of lightning—no, as fast as a firing synapse...

New equipment and the power of Divine Lion Protection... Thanks to these, Aria's power hasn't decreased at all. If anything, it's through the roof.

"Aria, you've at least built up some stamina over the past month, right?"

"Of course, Vulcan... Oh, I think I see what you're getting at!"

Vulcan addresses Aria joyfully as she whips her blade through the air to rid it of goblin blood.

Aria was about to inquire, *Why do you ask?* when she realizes her companion's intent.

Vulcan is proposing…a full-on assault on the labyrinth. Thanks to her new equipment and Tama's Divine Lion Protection, Aria is stronger than ever. Though her battle instincts may have dulled a bit, these two factors have compensated for that and then some.

In that case, rather than taking time to slowly get back in the saddle, Vulcan thinks Aria should fight as many battles as possible today and get her feet back under her as soon as possible.

Not to mention, she won't be fighting alone. Vulcan is an experienced vanguard who's also been strengthened by Tama's divine protection. Further, Tama is an elemental cat (or at least they think he is) who can take down multiple trolls all by his wee lonesome.

With Tama providing support for Aria and Vulcan, they shouldn't have any problem getting at least a few layers down…

It's been decided.

Hmm. I think it's best to recover gradually in stages…but my master and Vulcan are chomping at the bit. What can I say? I will support them to the fullest. If necessary, I can unleash all my skills, including Elemental Tail Blade, and destroy any enemy in our path.

Having reached that decision, Tama rubs his body against Aria's legs as if to put her at ease and nods with conviction, looking adorable all the while.

"Hee-hee, it seems Tama agrees!"

"Meown, in that case, we're as strong as an army of a hundred! Well, let's keep going… Wait, what's that?"

Aria picks up Tama, ever so cute and dependable, with a loving embrace and settles him between her breasts tightly. Vulcan responds by throwing a fist in the air to say, *In that case, nobody can stop us!*

As she pumps her fist, Vulcan's side boob becomes clearly visible as her supple, gorgeous underarm jiggles. In that moment…

Vulcan cries out in surprise, staring deep into the labyrinth. Aria notices it, too. At the back of the passage, a girl stands in the center, alone...

Whoa?! It's that aberrant maiden from last night!

Her sudden appearance shocks Tama to his core. There's no mistaking it—the girl standing there is the same one who demanded to copulate with him last night, chasing him around in her tattered tunic.

Hmm?! What's the meaning of this—? She looks different now. Almost like she's afraid of something...

Tama's body stiffens as he prepares for her to descend upon him like last night. But she defies his expectations.

The girl in the tattered tunic simply cries out softly, "Uhhhn...," as if terrified of something. Her anxious eyes are focused on Tama...or rather, on Aria, carrying Tama between her breasts.

"She can't be...an adventurer, can she? Why is someone dressed like that down in the labyrinth...?"

"Mm, and she looks terrified, doesn't she, meow? She's probably a vagabond who got herself lost down here."

Aria and Vulcan exchange opinions upon seeing the frightened girl in the tunic. She is beautiful, but her long flaxen hair is unkempt. She's half-naked—no surprise that one would take her for a vagabond.

Aria smiles sweetly at the girl and asks her a question.

"Hey, it's dangerous to be down here looking like that. Are you from Labyrinthos?"

Seeing someone in a place this dangerous without proper equipment and seemingly terrified, the noble Aria simply cannot ignore her, vagabond or not.

"...? I—I was born in the darkness... I don't know this place Labyrinthos, and I don't have any memory of ever being outside."

The girl in the tattered tunic looks different for a split second before responding to Aria's soft words in staggered, halted phrasing.

Hearing her, Aria and Vulcan glance at each other. This is not what they expected her to say.

"Vulcan, do you think she's...?"

"Meow, it's probably amnesia, you think?"

Even setting aside the fact that the labyrinth lies within the borders of the city of Labyrinthos, claiming to never have heard its name is inconceivable. What's more, the disheveled girl also claims to have no memory of ever being outside...

Aria and Vulcan have guessed that she's an adventurer who for one reason or another lost her memory in the labyrinth. The place is crawling with monsters, and while their types tend to be limited to certain levels of the labyrinth, it is possible—though rare—for more powerful ones to appear on the upper levels.

A number of adventurers have been known to suffer amnesia from the intense fear of being attacked by such a monster and having their lives put in mortal danger. It would not be entirely surprising if the girl in the tattered tunic has fallen under similar circumstances.

She looks terrified and has no memory—her fear might stem from the fact that she can't even tell left from right or vice versa... With this in mind, Aria addresses the girl again.

"At any rate, it's dangerous here. Please come back to the city with us."

"'*Back to the city*'...? I don't know what you're talking about, but I have some business with you... No, with the Fearsome Cat between your breasts...!"

"Fearsome Cat? Is she talking about Tama meow?"

"We just met you—how can you possibly know Tama is strong? And what business...?"

Although she still looks terrified, the girl now points at Tama, fully on guard as he rests between Aria's breasts after hearing his stalker's powerful challenge.

Aria and Vulcan only just met this girl, but she referred to Tama as the Fearsome Cat. Though puzzled, they nevertheless attempt to advance their dialogue.

But then...

"My purpose is to become one with the Fearsome Cat and bear his offspring! Come now, Fearsome Cat! Escape that female's bosom and KASPLOOSH your BABOOOOM inside my VAVAVOOM!!"

Whaaaaaaat the—?

The girl's cheeks flush, her breath ragged as she spews a bunch of nonsensical sounds. Tama is scared to death and clutches tightly to Aria's bosom.

Aria can't help but cry out in ecstasy, just a bit, but nonetheless...

"This is bad. She's obviously cracked her head on something, poor thing..."

"Meown. Definitely serious."

Aria and Vulcan both stare pityingly at the girl in the tattered tunic. In other words, they realize that, in addition to losing her memory, the girl isn't entirely right in the head.

"You know, it's not okay for a girl to shout something like that in public. Not to mention, Tama is still a kitten and can't even make babies yet. Please, let's just get out of here together, okay?"

"What say thee?! That the Fearsome Cat cannot conceive a child...? I don't understand whatsoever, but if I go with you, I will be able to be with the Fearsome Cat...?"

"Yes, Tama is my pet. If you come with us, you'll be alongside him, too!"

"Hmph, very well, I understand. I will join you!"

Aria nods and responds softly to the girl in the tunic's question. It goes without saying, though, that Aria would never surrender Tama, who she loves dearly, to some addled stranger treating her beloved companion like a piece of meat.

However, for the moment, ensuring this girl's safety is her top priority. If the girl wants to be near Tama, Aria will give her a brief taste of that reality to get her outside the labyrinth, first and foremost.

Aria's scheme is a success. Although she wavers for a moment, the girl in the tunic resolves to follow Aria and her party.

"Meown…? Aria, you're going to take care of this girl?"

"Of course I will, Vulcan. If she's lost her memories, then she obviously doesn't have anywhere to go. If that's the case, she could easily be forced into slavery."

Aria has already made up her mind to care for the girl in the tattered tunic for a while. She may look like a vagabond right now, but there's no doubt that her actual beauty would turn heads everywhere she went. She's quite buxom, too.

Her arms and legs are thin, but her thighs immediately connect with thick, juicy hips and a taut waist—her figure is plainly visible from underneath her shabby clothes. What's more—her breasts are extremely ripe and luscious, bouncing up and down with every movement she makes.

In terms of size, they're bigger than Vulcan's apples but smaller than Aria's melons…or thereabout. She looks approximately eighteen or nineteen years old. Her eyes pull you in, and when she stares at Tama excitedly, she appears hedonistic and lustful.

Throwing a girl like this from the labyrinth out on the street, she'll fall under the wretched watch of the wicked in no time. If that happens, she'll be captured and her body will be taken advantage of to no end.

What's more, a system of slavery exists in this world. Once someone is finished with or gets sick of you, you're done for. Being sold as a slave guarantees you will live day after day of hell on earth—thus Aria has decided to take the girl under her wing.

"Let's head to my lodging for now. I believe a more spacious room was available, so we'll switch to that one."

"I'll help, too. If you need anything, let me-ow know!"

Hearing Aria, Vulcan thumps her chest and declares that she, too, will lend a hand. Vulcan has a heightened sense of righteousness, just like Aria. This was proven during the quest to defeat the demon Beryl, when she joined Aria and company to protect the people of Renald, despite the danger involved.

Aria and Vulcan start heading for the exit outside. Following them, the girl in the tunic lags behind cautiously, still on her guard against Aria for some reason.

Hmm... Does this girl really have amnesia? If that's true, then I did something terrible last night. I should have at least adjusted my speed to lead her outside the labyrinth. But this feeling... I've felt it...somewhere before...

Despite the fact that this girl preyed upon him, aiming to steal his chastity, Tama pities her and rebukes himself for not considering her situation and leaving her in the labyrinth last night... Yet, at the same time, he doesn't trust her and can't escape the feeling that he's met her somewhere before.

"Okay, we've secured the double room, so let's go ahead and adjourn to the bath, shall we?"

"'*Bath*'...? What is that? Is it powerful?"

Aria and company have left the labyrinth and returned to the inn in the city. The innkeeper quickly prepared a double room for them after Aria explained the situation.

Vulcan is currently out choosing new clothing to replace the girl's tunic—at her own discretion—so she's not here.

Aria thought it would be best to get her guest cleaned up. She's downright filthy from her time in the labyrinth, and Aria suggested that she wash up...

...It seems, though, that the girl has lost her memory of even what a bath is. In her heart of hearts, Aria is having a hard time believing it.

"You see, the bath is where you go to wash your body clean with warm water. Do you remember experiencing anything like that? Um... By the way, what is your name?"

"Hmmmm...washing with water... I know of it, but I've never

done it myself. And I am strong...or rather, I once was. There is no other way to express myself."

"Is that so...? Well then, you definitely need a name! Is there anything you'd like to be called?"

"Hmph. I don't care at all what I'm called."

Aria feels compassion for the girl who doesn't even remember her own name. She brightly invited the girl to choose a name to her liking, even for the time being. Her response, though, was curt and cold.

The girl in the tattered tunic is now staring enraptured at Tama, who is seated quietly on the bed. He mews softly, seeing how she stares at him, and continues to observe her with a cautious expression.

"In that case, do you mind if I give you a name, even if it's temporary? Actually, I have one that suits you perfectly."

"Do as you like. I've already told you—I don't care what I'm called."

"Okay... From today, your name is Stella! It means *beautiful* in the land where I come from."

"Stella... I don't know what *beautiful* means, but the name does sound nice. If a woman such as yourself gives it to me, I have no complaint."

"Hee-hee, I'm so glad to hear that. We're really happy to have met you, Stella. ♪"

The girl in the tunic—rather, Stella—has granted a measure of respect to Aria, which she finds curious. At any rate, Stella seems to like her name, and the elf's face brightens immediately.

Hmm. Stella, is it? A fine name. My master has great taste across the board.

Tama mews in commendation of Aria's great naming sense. "Ohhh! Fearsome Cat! Your voice is as lovely as ever!" Stella replies as her cheeks flush and she begins panting.

Seeing her get excited, Tama once again recalls the fear of being chased for his chastity deep in the labyrinth. His body stiffens like a board, and he darts under the bed to hide.

"Wha—? Fearsome Cat, why do you run from me?! All I want is the seed of your fearsome being…"

That's exactly *what terrifies me! Uhhh… Master, please do something about this aberrant maiden…*

Stella poking her head under the bed and demanding that Tama impregnate her has him shaking like a leaf in a tornado as he silently pleads for Aria to intervene.

"Stop! That's not okay! Stella, you're scaring Tama… Like I said in the labyrinth, Tama's still a kitten. He can't make babies yet."

Seeing Tama obviously terrified, Aria quickly rushes to intervene. As his master and beloved, she has to protect his chastity from other girls.

Well, Aria also has the experience of running ahead full steam and nearly causing an incident with Tama…but let's forget about that for the time being.

"Ooooh… If you insist, I have no choice—I will give up for now."

Hearing Aria's rebuke, Stella reluctantly withdraws from under the bed.

Hmm. Just as I expected. Stella, for reasons I do not understand, listens to whatever master says.

Tama realizes that Stella either fears or respects Aria…or perhaps both at the same time. For this reason, if the command comes from Aria, she will accept it, although reluctantly, and cease whatever misbehavior in which she's engaged.

"Okay, let's go to the bath! The innkeeper filled it for us, so we're all set!"

Aria gathers herself and pushes everyone toward the bath. Stella responds enthusiastically to Aria's insistence. Seeing the strange girl brimming with curiosity, Aria is awash with emotion, realizing how childlike she really is.

At the same time, Aria detects a sense of purity and peril within Stella, seemingly a consequence of losing her memories. Aria's own sense of righteousness further compels her to watch over Stella carefully.

"Wow! What is this? Something is bubbling straight out of that rock!"

"That's called soap, and it's a tool used to wash your body, Stella. I'll wash you really well, so sit still for me, okay?"

Stella and Aria go back and forth in the hot-bath area of the inn, both as naked as the day they were born. Stella is entranced by the sudsy bar of soap in Aria's hand.

Hmm. I can't bear looking at any girl aside from my master naked, but there's nothing I can do about this...

Tama resolves himself as he watches the two girls from the corner of the bath.

Aria invites him to join them. "Tama, let's get you all clean, too, okay?"

However, the behemoth cub is wary. *There's no way I can get in the bath with this lunatic...!*

But it's no use...

Wait a second! This aberrant maiden may be abiding my master now, but isn't it too early to trust her?! There's no telling when she'll run amok and lash out at Aria. As her knight, I must be here to protect her.

Tama decides to get in the bath, if only for the sake of protecting Aria as her pet (knight).

"Wow! The dirt on my body is disappearing by the second! That soap you speak of is quite the tool!"

Stella can't contain her excitement as Aria washes her body clean. She's really riled up, and her breasts are bouncing up and down with abandon.

"Okay, I'm done washing your body, so now let's do your hair. It will hurt if soap gets in your eyes, so shut them tight, okay?"

"Wha—?! I do not want my eyes in pain! I will not open them!"

Hearing Aria caution her, Stella reacts...or rather, completely freaks out and shuts her eyes as tight as she can. Has she endured a particular pain to her eyes in the past? Aria wonders as much and worries as she gently washes her hair.

"Ooooh... Aren't you done yet?"

"Hee-hee, once I rinse with warm water, you'll be done. Almost there!"

In response to Stella's frightened tone, Aria scoops water from the bath with a wooden bucket and slowly pours it over Stella's head to rinse away the suds.

"Wow! What is this sensation?! I feel refreshed!"

After her hair is rinsed, Stella once again erupts with excitement. Now that her filthy body is washed clean, having never had the experience of bathing, her deep emotion is understandable.

"Now that we're done washing, let's move to the other bath and go for a soak to warm ourselves up! ♪"

"'Go for a soak'...? You mean get in this hot water? Why would you ever...?"

"It's very important for human beings, especially girls, to warm their bodies, Stella."

"Ooooh? I don't understand, but if you insist, I will follow suit... Wow, this feels amazing!"

Stella doesn't grasp the importance of soaking in hot water, but she follows Aria's lead anyway. She's once again highly impressed.

"Now it's your turn, Tama!"

"Meown—!"

Aria kneels down in the bath and calls to Tama. He responds enthusiastically and starts trotting toward her before jumping up onto her knees and flopping over onto his back, belly up.

Aria always starts washing Tama from his fluffy li'l tummy, and he naturally assumes the position. For the record...from this position, Tama can see Aria's gorgeous face peeking out perfectly from between her two melons.

The resplendent view excited him beyond measure when he first started living with Aria, and even now, it still gets him going.

"N-not fair! I want to wash the Fearsome Cat's body, too!"

As Tama is being washed by Aria's loving hand and thinking, *Heaven... This is heaven...*, Stella stands up in a rush, causing a huge splash, and complains to Aria, jealousy painted on her face.

"Hee-hee, no, no, Stella. Washing Tama is a special privilege for me, his master. I have no intention of ever letting you have a turn."

Aria is sweeter than syrup. It isn't unreasonable to assume she might pass Tama over and share him, but her response is a surprising "absolutely not."

On any given day, Aria has three special sources of satisfaction that she will not give up—and for good reason. The first is washing Tama and playing with him in the bath.

Consequently, even if the childish Stella insists, Aria has zero intention of letting her.

"Ohhh, Fearsome Cat, you are so lovely! Just looking at you makes me throb! Uhhhhng!!"

Stella has her hand cupped over her private parts and her cheeks are flushed red—utterly carnal. Her voice is strained as she stares at Aria and Tama with intense jealousy during their "feline fun time" bathing ritual.

"Huh? What is this smell? It's making me hungry as hell!"

Aria and company have returned from the bath to their room at the inn. Vulcan has completed her shopping, and when Stella puts on the clothes prepared for her, she can't believe how good they feel.

It is at that moment...Stella looks around the room and starts sniffing the air like a hound.

"I think you're smelling smoked skirt steak. It's almost time for dinner—we should eat, too."

"'*Smoked skirt steak*'...? That is the source of this scent? How can I get it in my mouth? Do I need to defeat the smoked skirt steak in battle?"

The source of the aroma is smoke rising from the first-floor bar at the inn, where their house special smoked meat is being prepared.

"Don't worry meow, Stella! You don't have to defeat any enemies to eat dinner, so settle down."

"Hee-hee, you're so riled up at the smell of meat… You are too darn cute, Stella."

Stella was living in complete survival mode in the labyrinth before she met Aria and company. With her memories gone, it's unsurprising that she thinks you have to defeat a creature in order to eat it. Realizing this, Vulcan gently soothes her, assuring the girl that nothing of that sort will be required.

Aria finds her guest absolutely adorable, and even though Stella looks older than her, Aria is reminded that she's just a child inside.

"Stella seems really interested, so let's have dinner at the bar on the first floor tonight! ♪ Vulcan, you'll join us, right?"

"Of course meow! The food here is damn near as good as the guild!"

Vulcan picks up Tama standing at her feet and holds him in her breasts, eagerly accepting Aria's invitation.

Stella rushes Aria with stars in her eyes, saying, "If I follow you, I'll be able to devour the source of this smell! Hurry up, now!"

Just as Aria suspected all along, Stella is like a little sister— innocence personified.

Tama and the trio of girls trot down the stairs to the inn's bar. A few minutes after being seated, a line of drool streams from Stella's mouth onto the table. She clearly can't wait to devour meat as its delicious aroma wafts her way.

Aria and Vulcan, sitting across from her, look a bit tired. Understandable given that, just moments after their arrival, Stella saw food sitting on another table and screamed, "These are myyyyy spoils!!" while accosting the other patrons.

Aria and Stella rushed to stop her from causing a scene. However, Stella resisted fiercely, and they were put in the awkward situation of wrestling her to calm her down, which inevitably wore them out.

Stella has no memory of how to wait for your food at a restaurant, either. Judging from the way she was talking on the second floor, they should have predicted as much but had come down unprepared.

Stella is gripping her fork with a tight fist and stabs down through the air, drool streaming from her mouth. Aria, anticipating that Stella probably doesn't know how to use silverware, either, begins explaining how to at least use a fork while they await the arrival of their meal.

Stella's initial response is, "Why do I have to use this thing to eat?"

However, Aria tells her, "You're a girl, and if you can't use silverware properly, none of the boys will like you..."

"What! That cannot happen! My goal is to become one with the Fearsome Cat! I cannot be disliked by him!"

In a huff, Stella quickly begins practicing how to use the fork.

"Gah-ha-ha! How about it, Fearsome Cat? I can use a fork. I'm quite the catch, aren't I?"

Making poking motions with her fork, Stella looks downright triumphant.

Ensconced in Aria's breasts, Tama experiences another flash of déjà vu and thinks, *I've heard that laugh somewhere before...*

"Sorry to keep you waiting! One order of smoked skirt steak. I'll bring everything else out, too—just a minute."

The landlady of the inn's hands are occupied with a huge plate full of smoked meat that smells absolutely delicious.

"Wow!! So much tasty-smelling meat! Can I eat now?!"

"Yes, Stella, eat as much as you want."

"Yes!! Wh-what is this?! I've never tasted meat so delicious!"

Stella instantly rips into the food. Moments later, the delicious flavor and smoky goodness filling her mouth cause her to erupt in shock. Now her mind is free.

Stella has been rendered incapable of anything other than stabbing a piece of meat, delivering it to her mouth, and repeating indefinitely.

"Meown—! She's really going at it! Where is all that going to fit in her tiny tummy?"

Vulcan is even more shocked watching Stella eat than Stella herself was at the meat's deliciousness. Unsurprising, given that—unassisted—Stella has devoured the entire mountain of steak mere moments after its arrival.

"Okay, here's your sausage platter and house salad... Wait, you finished the steak already?!"

The innkeeper brings out the rest of their food. She can't hide her surprise that the smoked skirt steak, which completely filled the plate, has disappeared in just a few minutes.

"Ohhh! That meat smells really good, too! Can I eat it?"

"Of course, Stella. But you have to eat your vegetables, too, okay?"

"'Vegetables'...? Are you talking about that grass? Do humans eat grass?"

Vegetables, too, have slipped out of Stella's memory, it would seem. Aria explains the importance of eating vegetables, including how dressing makes them taste delicious... At that point, she pushes some toward Stella and...

"...!! Wow! Vegetables! Not as good as meat but pretty tasty! I could eat this all day!"

Stella digs into the salad with gusto. Aria is relieved she wasn't picky about it. She's already treating Stella like a real caregiver would.

"Okay, Tama, let's get you some food, too."

"Meown—!"

Keeping one eye on Stella stuffing her cheeks with sausage and salad, Aria pushes a piece of sausage on her fork toward Tama. He mews happily and bites down on it. *Chomp—!* His bite makes a satisfying sound as the sausage is torn off the fork. Delicious juice and rich flavor fill Tama's mouth.

All the food here is made to order in-house, the spices carefully selected. Sausage happens to be one of Tama's favorite things in the world.

He looks adorable as he savors the taste with his cheeks stuffed.

"Awww… Tama is just the absolute cutest. ♡"

"Meowwww—my heart is throbbing just watching him."

Entranced by Tama's cuteness, Aria starts rubbing her thighs together. Vulcan is also hot and bothered as her cheeks flush red.

"Wh-what is this?! I didn't know the Fearsome Cat could be so extremely cute! I must make an offering to him, too!"

Stella rushes to chew the multiple sausages she'd stuffed into her mouth, swallowing them before skewering another on her fork and pushing it toward Tama, who simply looks the other way.

Stella is shocked. "Wha…?! Why, Fearsome Cat? Why do you turn away from me?!"

Obviously, because I don't trust you at all yet. You went after my chastity—what did you expect?

Tama's guard is still up. Aside from the aforementioned reason, he simply smells danger on Stella. It might be his instincts as a monster or intuition stemming from his past life as a knight.

Huh…? I wonder what's happened—it's so rare for Tama to behave like that toward a person.

Aria can't help feeling something is off about Tama's reaction.

The kitten is gentle and very friendly. He's generally quick to warm up to Aria's acquaintances, but he hasn't dropped his guard around Stella whatsoever.

Being this on edge is like poison to him. With that thought, Aria picks him up.

Boing—!

Tama jumps up and burrows in between Aria's breasts.

Instantly, the other customers—mostly men—start murmuring among themselves. Aria's melons and the cat poking his face out from between them...the visual is overwhelming, and some respond with gratitude, saying, "Good boy, good boy," while others snarl with jealousy. "You little prick! Trade places with me now!"

Ahhh... It's warm and smells so good between her breasts...

Tama's fur was standing on end from the agitation, but reminded of Aria's maternal affection by her scent and warmth, he finally relaxes.

Meown—Aria, I'm so jealous! I want to seduce Tama with meown boobs, too!

Vulcan has tiger DNA in her veins and is quite attracted to a strong cat such as Tama. It's not surprising she feels that way about him.

"Damn it! Damn it! If I wasn't eating, I would do something about this!"

Stella is jealous and annoyed that Tama ran from her but is stuck to Aria like glue. In the end, she gets desperate and orders another mountain of smoked skirt steak and sausages.

"Ugh...I can't move a muscle. This is pain."

"That should be obvious—you ate so much. You have to control yourself, Stella, okay?"

The crew is back in their room on the second floor of the inn, where Stella moans painfully.

Her face looks terrible. No wonder—she ate more than is conceivable, all by herself...

Stella refused to listen when Aria tried to stop her. Though generally reticent and calm, the elf now can't help but look miffed.

Stella's other caretaker, Vulcan, said good-bye downstairs and has already gone home.

"I'm not sure if you'll be able to brush your teeth. Oh well—we might as well go to bed tonight."

"Uhhh...'brush teeth'? I don't know what that means, but I am not fit for any further activity today. I shall sleep. Where do I lay my body?"

"Oh the bed, of course... Wait, you don't even remember beds, do you? Stella, over here."

Seeing how Stella reacts quizzically to even the word *bed*, Aria takes her by the hand and leads her to one of the two beds.

"Wow! Lying here is so comfortable! This is a first— Oof, I can't say any more. I must sleep..."

Stella is quite moved by how comfortable the bed is, but when she lies down, intense nausea racks her, causing her to fall silent.

"Okay, Tama, let's brush our teeth and go to bed, too. ♪"

"Meown—!"

Glancing at Stella, now mute, Aria calls Tama and hugs him between her breasts, heading for the corner of the room. Even though the hotel is cheap, it has a sink in every room. The sink in theirs has a cup and a toothbrush, along with a super-tiny toothbrush, waiting above it. The former is, of course, Aria's, and the latter, Tama's. Aria had the tiny toothbrush custom-made, and she brushes his teeth with it every day.

"Ooh... You're shunning me and flirting with the Fearsome Cat again..."

Stella's voice floats like a jealous curse in the air, but Aria is absorbed in brushing Tama's teeth and doesn't hear her. Rather, she's thinking, heart pounding, *Awww! Tama is so darn cute when he sits still to have his teeth brushed!* ♡

Mmmm. This vibrating sensation feels so good. My master's technique is so skillful, as always.

Tama is replete with satisfaction at how good Aria's gentle, skilled teeth cleansing feels. Aria continues brushing her own teeth and squeezes Tama tight as she sits on the bed.

As she does, she hears Stella's jealous curse this time. "N-not fair! You get to sleep with the Fearsome Cat... Ugh..."

Sleeping with Tama is Aria's last source of satisfaction for the day. It's something she simply can't give up.

"Good night! ♪" Aria says to Stella in a singsong voice and strokes Tama lovingly before falling fast asleep.

In the middle of the night—

—*Hey. Get up, Fearsome Cat...*

Tama hears a voice inside his head as he gently snores, tucked in between Aria's breasts.

Am I...hearing things?

Or is it a dream? Tama looks sleepy as he ponders the mysterious voice that directly entered his brain.

—*Ohhh! Finally, I can speak to you! I see—it appears I can reach you via "conversation"!*

What the...?!

The voice continues ringing in Tama's head. It's not some sort of auditory hallucination or dream. He instinctively opens his eyes.

—*You are awake, Fearsome Cat! Now then, we have much to discuss!*

In addition to her resounding voice, Stella appears at the foot of the bed, looking sorrowful.

My god, it was Stella all along...?

Tama's consciousness is alerted by her "conversation," still audible.

Stella stands before him. The voice he hears is distinctly hers. *It can't be...*, Tama thinks when he suddenly has a premonition.

—That's right! I am speaking to you through telepathy. All you have to do is think, and I can understand what you are saying!

Tama's premonition is correct, and as the Stella in front of him nods deeply, he hears her voice in his head at the same time.

A telepathic skill... I've heard rumors of it before, but to actually see it happening... This can't be good! Everyone thinks I'm a cat, but if I can understand human language—even if it's telepathy—that could cause a host of problems...!

The rare skill of telepathy exists in this world. Tama is quite impressed that Stella possesses it, but more importantly, he realizes how crucial this moment is. Though through telepathy, Stella now knows that Tama can participate in conversation. If she takes this information and tells Aria...

His master will be perplexed by his level of intelligence and then possibly realize his identity as a former human reincarnated—what's more, the fact that he's not a cat at all but an S-ranked monster. A behemoth...

Just imagining it sends a jolt down Tama's spine.

—Why so flustered, Fearsome Cat? You spoke with such a deafening roar as you slaughtered me, did you not?

.........Huh?

This... She... Stella, what is she talking about? I slaughtered her? Tama's mind is thrown into further confusion.

The little behemoth certainly has no memory of killing a beautiful girl like Stella, and even if he did, why would she be standing here if she'd been murdered? As Tama contemplates this...

—What?!?! Do you really not know who I am? In the bowels of the labyrinth, you fought me on two different occasions, finally transforming into a colossal lacquer-black entity and rupturing my head with a massive flaming greatsword! And in that moment, you said you were a behemoth, *did you not?*

What the—?!

Tama's eyes grow wide. Hearing Stella's words, the memory of a certain day rushes to his mind. Just one month ago...Aria had fallen to the poison of the demon Beryl's blade, and to find the ingredient necessary to create an antidote to purify that poison—to secure the eye of an earth dragon—Tama confronted an earth dragon alone.

In the middle of that lengthy, horrendous battle...Tama realized he was outmatched by the beast. Even realizing that he wouldn't be able to return to his former self, he evolved into the second stage of his behemoth form, and just like Stella said, he'd used a massive flaming sword—Flame Edge—to successfully come out on top.

What's more, Tama had also experienced battle with the earth dragon shortly after being reincarnated, when he touched a Warp Crystal and was transported on top of the dragon's head, angering it deeply.

Stella directly referenced these situations in which he'd found himself and knows there were two battles... Given the scope of information, Tama can't help but think...

Is it...? No...unfathomable—!!

—Gah-ha-haaa! You have remembered! That's right—I am the dragon you defeated in the labyrinth...in my reincarnated form!

A piercing sneer erupts in Tama's mind alongside the shocking truth. Hearing this, Tama recognizes and comprehends what's happening.

The déjà vu he'd felt around Stella was not a misunderstanding. She is the very earth dragon he killed just one month earlier...

The reality that the earth dragon, which he definitely killed, has changed her appearance to stand in front of him, coupled with the fact that Stella used the phrase *"reincarnated form,"* has him totally convinced.

It's said that high-level dragons endlessly repeat a cycle of transmigration, retaining the same memory over the course of thousands of years. Tama has also heard that they occasionally reincarnate as other species.

As he recalls the legends surrounding dragons, Stella tells him through telepathy, *After you defeated me, my consciousness fell again into darkness—I awoke deep in the labyrinth. I understood that I had reincarnated into a human being's body through the ancient skill Reincarnation, which I possessed in my dragon form...*

—What is it you want, earth dragon? To take your revenge on me? In that case, be my guest!

Tama crawls out from between Aria's breasts and sharply narrows his normally adorable eyes, staring at Stella—at the earth dragon—and bristling the fur on his back.

Although reincarnated as a cute girl, Stella is a once-fearsome enemy he's defeated. There's no reason her heart wouldn't be filled with the desire for revenge.

—W-wait, Fearsome Cat! I was defeated by you, and I surrender. I have no intention of fighting!

—Wh-what? Well then, what do you want?

—I've already told you! My goal is to mate with you, a fearsome male, and produce offspring! The first time I realized your true power, I knew you were the right male to impregnate me. So...

—Come KASPLOOSH your BABOOOOM inside my VAVAVOOOOOOM!!!

"Meowwwwn!!" *Oh my god! This lady is twisted!!*

Stella raises her voice within the telepathic communication and rushes to maul Tama. Absolutely terrified, he cries out. The blood-curdling yowl of a kitten echoes throughout the Labyrinthos night.

"No! You're scaring Tama! Don't be rough with him, Stella!"

"Eek—?!"

Stella spews off a string of disturbing exclamations as she prepares to dive on top of Tama.

I have nowhere to run. This is the end...

Tama looks largely defeated. Just then, Aria's voice breaks through Tama and Stella's scuffle. She's been awakened by Tama's cry of terror.

The second she hears Aria's voice, Stella performs the superhuman feat of a midair about-face before rushing to the corner of the room, where she's shaking like a leaf. It seems she's still scared of Aria.

"Meown—!" *Master!*

Tama is at his wits' end. Seeing Aria there to save him, his face lights up, and he dives directly back into her cleavage.

"Hee-hee, you're okay now, right, Tama?"

"Meown..."

Aria holds Tama close and strokes him ever so softly. Relieved by her comforting touch, his eyes narrow in satisfaction.

"Stella, I know that Tama is very alluring, but like I told you earlier, he's just a kitten and can't make babies. More than anything, he's my pet, and I have no intention of ever giving him to you. Got it?"

"Unnngh... It's not fair... But I..."

Aria's voice is sweet, but she's reprimanding Stella harshly. The former earth dragon mumbles in frustration and drags herself back to the bed.

Aria sighs in relief and returns to her own bed to mull over how to handle this going forward. "If this sort of thing keeps happening, I'll have to come up with a solution..."

—*Hey, Fearsome Cat. I'll give up for today, but listen well: I am absolutely in love with you...!*

"..."

Stella's telepathy echoes in Tama's mind as he burrows deeply into Aria's breasts.

Tama can only remain silent at this sudden confession of love.

The next morning:

"What is this?! Last night's smoked steak and sausage platter were delicious, but this is also amazing!"

In the cafeteria on the first floor of the inn, Stella is just as excited as she was at dinner yesterday. She's completely forgotten how upset Aria got with her in the middle of the night.

In Stella's hand is a fragrant piece of toast covered in crispy bacon and a soft-boiled egg.

"And this *fruity water* you gave me is amazing! I've never drunk such delicious water before!"

As she nibbles on her toast, Stella intermittently takes sips of her fruit juice and shouts enthusiastically.

Although Aria's guard has been up a bit since last night, seeing Stella act like a child, she feels like any poison that was present has been sucked out. Suddenly, she turns to her and says, "Stella, it might be rude of me to ask you this because you don't have any memories, but is there anything you're especially good at?"

"Mmmph—? Something I'm good at?"

Stella was reaching for another piece of toast when she hears Aria's question and stops dead in her tracks.

Aria's been thinking about something since last night. Taking care of Stella doesn't particularly bother her, since it was her idea to begin with. That said, there's no guarantee Stella's memories will ever return.

In that case, Aria will need to train her so she can live on her own and find a job… To that end, above all else, she wants Stella to learn the meaning of "he who does not work, neither shall he eat."

In response to Aria's posing of the aphorism and her question, Stella replies, "Well, I'm good at fighting! No—if anything, I actually love it!"

"Fighting… I see. But wait—Stella, you were so scared in the labyrinth, right? If you like fighting, isn't that a little weird?"

"What say thee? That was simply me being afraid of you. I was not afraid of any monsters or of fighting itself!"

"Wha—?! Afraid of me? Why would you say that, Stella? I don't recall ever doing anything to you…?"

"It's true that I have no experience of ill intentions at your hand. Yet, the Fearsome Cat bends to your will like a child. How ridiculous of you to claim that I should not be afraid of a being such as yourself!"

Aria is noticeably shocked at the fact that Stella was actually afraid of her. Tama also thinks, *Ohhh…I get it…*from his spot tucked into Aria's cleavage.

In other words, Stella both respects and fears Aria because she is the master of Tama, her pet (knight), who previously defeated the former earth dragon in a single fell swoop.

The world of monsters is eat or be eaten. Weaklings are devoured by the powerful or made their slaves. Aria hasn't simply subjugated or controlled Tama; she loves him like a child.

Unable to ascertain the true power of someone that unfeasibly strong, Stella was understandably terrified.

—Hey, Fearsome Cat. Just who is this girl Aria? She has subjugated you and all your incredible power, yet she's wrapped in an aura of gentleness. It doesn't make any sense.

As Tama finally understands Stella's inexplicable reaction to Aria and comes to terms with it, Stella enters his head telepathically.

—*She is many things to me: my benefactor, my beloved master. She is a kind human. That's why she's looking after a wayward creature like you. You better watch yourself moving forward.*

—*I can't believe that you, most Fearsome Cat, can call her master... Ugggh! Such an incredible female! I'm shivering!*

In response to Stella's telepathic outreach, Tama tested his ability to push his words onto her. In response, her voice again erupted in his head. It appears his use of telepathy was on point.

—*By the way, earth dragon...erm, Stella. You must never tell my master that I can use telepathy like this.*

—*Hmm? And why is that? It would benefit you greatly to be able to express your thoughts with words to communicate.*

—*My master doesn't know that I'm an S-ranked behemoth—she's mistaken me as a very powerful cat. As her knight, it benefits me to maintain that perception.*

—*Ohhh really? That's a tasty bit of information. Fearsome Cat, if you don't want her to find out, you must pledge to copulate with me!*

—*Wha—?!*

Tama is too shocked for words at Stella's demand. He did not think that a former monster would resort to blackmail.

—*...That was a joke, I'm afraid. My sense of pride will not allow me to compel you, whom I love deeply, into becoming mine. Fearsome Cat, in the end, I will win you over. Prepare yourself for that day!*

—*...I can't believe that you, a former monster, would joke like that... But never mind this idea of winning me over. For now, I can't have you calling me Fearsome Cat all the time. Please call me Tama, just as my master does.*

—*Ohhh! You'll allow me to address you by name? Excellent—this is a step forward.*

Tama hasn't let his guard down. However, their conversation

thus far has revealed that Stella harbors no animosity toward him. He now understands that she's in love with him.

The little cat can't reciprocate her feelings, but even so, he's decided to take one step closer to her, given that they'll be living together from now on.

And although he only did it to save his master, he does feel guilty—albeit slightly—for taking Stella's life in the first place. Perhaps that's another reason.

Huh, that's weird... It's like Tama and Stella are somehow communicating with each other...

As Aria watches them converse silently via telepathy, she gets an intuitive sense of this and feels a pang of jealousy.

"Meown... Stella, are you sure that's what you want to wear?"

"Of course I am! It suits me perfectly!"

At Vulcan's item shop, a mid-level establishment in a corner of the city, Stella responds to Vulcan's question with the cheerfulness of a confident girl.

Stella told Aria during breakfast that she's good at fighting, prompting the elf to ask if she wanted to become an adventurer. Stella replied with an enthusiastic "Yes, I do!"

Aria suspected Stella was just blowing hot air, given her lack of memory...but then, showing off her knowledge, Stella said, "Adventurers are humans who defeat monsters in return for money!"

Ever since her life as an earth dragon began, Stella already had a certain level of knowledge about this world. She also had experience fighting those calling themselves adventurers in the labyrinth. She often thought their lifestyle looked enjoyable and yearned for something similar. As such, she was very happy with Aria's proposal.

"But, Stella, if you're going to wear that, then you should at least equip some gauntlets, don't you think?"

Stella looks quite pleased with herself in her adventurer's outfit, but Vulcan skeptically suggests putting on more gear.

Stella's outfit is very high on the revealing scale. Her top is nothing but a piece of leather cloth, showing all her cleavage and under boob. On the bottom, she's wearing only hot pants.

Both items are undersize and very low-rise. From the front, the area of coverage resembles a swimsuit at best. From behind, it's far more provocative. The top half of her plump butt cheeks are more or less hanging out on full display.

The hot pants in question were a normal design pattern to begin with, but when Stella tried them on, she said, "I need them to cover less area so I can show more! Cut off half the back portion covering my butt!" The end result is as present.

"I want leg protection, but I don't need any for my arms!"

"...And why is that, Stella? You don't want gauntlets, but you want leggings...?"

Stella's response to the suggestion is confusing. Aria quizzically presses further, to which Stella replies:

"Hmm? It will be faster to show you than tell you. This is what I'm talking about!"

Stella grunts softly, "Hnnngh!" with a show of effort. Now what's going on...?

Stella's whole body, including her chest and rear, is wrapped in a soft light. As it grows brighter, it also extends its scope.

A few seconds later, the light stops shining and...

What the—?! What is this?

"She has dragon arms and a tail, oh meow goodness!"

"Incredible! Stella, did you used to be a dragonewt?"

Tama, Vulcan, and Aria can't hide their surprise. Just as Vulcan said, Stella's arms have expanded to four times their normal size into giant earth-colored appendages. They are thick and appear reptilian.

Her hands have grown as well, with sharp claws extending from her fingertips. Also, Stella has a thick tail growing from the part

of her rear end sticking out of her hot pants. It's muscular like her arms and similarly reptilian.

As for what a "dragonewt" is—in this world, there exists a species of demi-humans that have dragon blood running in them. They are called dragonewts.

At first glance, they don't look any different from other human races, but this species in particular can turn certain parts of their bodies into dragons on command. Attacks delivered by these appendages are extremely powerful.

Aria has heard rumors that they can crush boulders with their bare hands. Both she and Vulcan are now convinced—Stella was able to survive in the labyrinth after losing her memory because she's a dragonewt.

In reality…Aria and company are still mistaken regarding Stella's amnesia.

"*'Dragon newt'*? I don't know what that is, but just looking at me is proof of my power!"

The strength of Stella's half-dragon body was bestowed on her when she reincarnated from a dragon. For this reason, she is not a member of the dragonewt race that Aria is talking about.

At least, she shouldn't be… But looking at her, Tama can't help but wonder.

…She looks exactly like the dragonewts I saw in my past life. Perhaps dragonewts are what dragons become when they reincarnate or the descendants of such beings…?

Tama has experience with dragonewts from his past life. Specifically, he worked alongside one. There was a female dragonewt in his knight squadron.

During battle, she wielded a giant battle-ax in her arms, which turned into those of a dragon, just like Stella's. Her power was unfathomable.

She and Tama were partners. Through her indomitable strength and Tama's colorful array of swordsmanship skills, praises were sung among the squadron for the pair's sheer might.

Come to think of it, she also wore a very suggestive outfit to allow her body to transform into a dragon, just like Stella.

Tama is absorbed in nostalgic recollections of their time on the battlefield as he recalls his former partner's outfits. She also wore skimpy armor that revealed her cleavage and rear end...

"Well, I guess that solves the mystery of your fashion choice, Stella!"

"Meown, okay, you have your adventurer outfit; now you need a weapon! What sort do you wanna try, Stella?"

"Ohhh! A weapon. Weapons are like swords and staffs, right?"

Stella's eyes light up when she hears the word *weapon*. She was always curious about the ones she saw adventurers using during her time as a dragon and wanted to try her hand at it. Now that she finally has the chance to do so, she can't contain her excitement.

"I'd like to go for a sword... But first, I think I want *that*!"

Stella starts walking through the shop in search of something. Vulcan asks her what she has in mind and begins showing her around but stops short after seeing Stella eagerly searching high and low, like a child hunting for treasure.

Getting Stella to answer her would only spoil the girl's fun. Aria can feel Vulcan holding back and watches Stella with a loving gaze.

"Found it! This is what I want to try first!"

Stella gives a shout from the back of the shop. When Aria and company reach her, they realize she's in the shield section. She's standing in the center of the area holding something and looking very proud.

"Meown?! Meow wow! She's lifting a black iron greatshield with one hand!"

"Wait—are my eyes deceiving me...? Stella, you deactivated your dragon body, right?"

Is she really holding up a black iron greatshield with one hand?! What kind of infernal strength...?!

Stella hoists a greatshield easily as tall as she is. And this is no average greatshield. It shines a piercing silvery black. This bright flash is the sign of the metal known as black iron, famous for its extreme weight. Stella has deactivated her dragon body without telling anyone, but she's still holding up the shield with her delicate and dainty doll arms.

Looking closely, Tama can see she does appear to be struggling a bit, but a normal human simply cannot wield a shield of this heft. Vulcan's, Aria's, and Tama's flabbergasted expressions are completely understandable.

There's no denying that, even without her dragon body, Stella has incredible inherent physical strength.

"I'm purrfectly surprised… I can't believe that another person would appear who can wield that shield other than Sakura…"

"Oh, is that the same greatshield Sakura used?"

"Yes, that's the one…the Mega Shield. When she got pregnant with Maiya's child and retired as an adventurer, she left it here at the shop."

The obsidian shield in question—the Mega Shield Vulcan's referencing—was an article used by Sakura, the former captain of the same knight squadron to which Cedric and company are now attached. She was also a member of Vulcan's adventurer party.

"Sakura had the high-level skill Iron Wall. It negated all nonfatal damage and nulled the weight of any weapons. What incredible effects."

"I see—that skill led to her being praised as the greatest tank warrior in the whole city."

As Vulcan, beaming brightly, reminisces about her former partner, Aria can see the logic behind her story.

Casting a sidelong glance at Aria and Vulcan, Tama secretly turns to speak to Stella.

—*You really surprised me, Stella. You're so bloodthirsty, I thought you would go for a sword or ax, not fly toward the shields…*

—*Ohhh! Tama! It pleases me greatly that you have engaged me* in telepathy first. I was never interested in shields before I reincarnated, but I learned the importance of defense during our last fight together. Had I had a means of defense at that time, I could have defeated you…or maybe not, but I could have at least likely survived.

—…I see. Your interest in shields stems from the fear instilled in you by my final death blow…

—Hmph! Ridiculous, isn't it? This proud dragon is now a small girl who's afraid of her enemies' attacks. Laugh at me all you like.

—What are you saying? Being afraid of enemy attacks is a given. Your senses were completely skewed up until now. You should be thankful that you learned the importance of defense… And look, it's me, who defeated you, telling you such a thing…

—Mmmm? Are you fretting over the fact that you killed me? Don't worry about it. It doesn't bother me—if anything, I must thank thee! I've learned of my true strength, and of love, because of you! And I've been able to take the form of a human being to meet you again!

—Um…well, as long as you're happy, I guess.

Hearing Stella confess her love once again, Tama falls silent before saying more, just like last night.

Tama can't deny Stella's feelings to her face because of his guilt over killing her and the fact that her affection for him is so direct.

"I can move freely in this outfit, and I have defensive capabilities… Now I finally need a weapon! Ohhh! This one looks great!"

After one-sidedly foisting her affections on Tama, Stella's expression morphs back into that of a giddy child as she rushes over to the sword section.

She picks up an affordable blade and slashes it through the air excitedly. Tama can't help but chuckle silently.

The first level of the labyrinth—

"Gah-ha-ha! I can't wait to use my weapon in battle!"

Stella is in high spirits as she laughs loudly in the dimly lit caverns. She's holding the obsidian greatshield—the Mega Shield—in her left hand. In her right, she grasps a greatsword of the same silvery black hue.

Stella has chosen a greatsword as her weapon. It is even more massive than a buster sword. It's as long as she is tall, and the blade is exceptionally wide.

As opposed to cutting down foes, her weapon is best suited to smashing them into pancakes.

Stella looks cool as a cucumber wielding the massive defensive armament and heavy weapon, even though she's not in her dragon form. How much power does she hold in that tiny frame?

But moving right along...

After Stella finished choosing her equipment, the party arrived at the labyrinth in the early morning. Thinking of Stella's physical condition—she'd been found in the labyrinth only a few days ago—Aria'd proposed, "Let's get you all equipped today and start actual adventurer activities in a few days." However...

"What? Why—? Now that I'm finally equipped, it's not fair to postpone actual battle! I want to use my weapon and fight as soon as possible!"

...Stella threw a tantrum. If she really felt that way, then Aria and Vulcan had no cause to stop her. In that case, it seemed best to let her get used to her new weapon today, allowing them to gauge her actual power.

For this reason, they've arrived at the labyrinth without taking on a particular quest... In fact, Aria hasn't completely regained her own battle instincts yet, making this the most reasonable course of action.

"Tama, first we'll let Stella put on a full display of her power. For now, please don't use any buff skills."

"Meown—!" *Yes, master!*

In order to fully ascertain Stella's capabilities, Aria orders Tama to refrain from activating Divine Lion Protection, and he mews obediently. However, Aria also quietly asks him, "If a dangerous situation arises, please protect Stella, too, okay?"

My former most powerful adversary is now the object of my protection... There's no telling how the tables will turn in this life.

With that in mind, Tama nods profusely in response to Aria, as if to say, *You got it!*

"Ohhh! Tama will protect me...? That's so reassuring—I'm touched!"

Stella has never had the experience of being protected, and if the male with whom she first fell in love after being born—Tama—is going to protect her, she's justifiably emotional.

"We'll start out by going after some moderate enemies, okay meow?!"

On Vulcan's command, the party sets off into the depths of the labyrinth.

"Gu-gi—!"

A few minutes after delving inside—

Vulcan leads the party forward as a grotesque being appears before them with a grating screech. It's a goblin, the type of monster guaranteed to appear on the first level.

The creature is outnumbered, and its physicality and equipment don't hold a candle to Aria and company. Nevertheless, it rushes them with dagger in hand, screaming, *"Gu-gyaaaa—!"*

Tama's appearance would lead you to think he's dead meat. The goblin looks at Aria, Vulcan, and Stella—three gorgeous girls—as potential wet mothers for its offspring, unable to conceal its lust.

Goblins are dumb as bricks. When their lust surges, they can't gauge how weak they are compared to their opponent, including difference in strength or numbers.

"Gah-ha-ha-ha! This little demon doesn't know its place! You dare to attack the likes of me? How incredible! Let your blood taint my blade!"

Stella cackles maniacally. She looks feral, an expression of heinous dreadfulness painted across her face.

Aria and Vulcan had been treating Stella as a child, but seeing her expression now, they can feel a cold chill running up their spines. Tama, on the other hand, recognizes this behavior: *Ah yes, this is the earth dragon I knew...*

"Now!"

The goblin approaches Stella, whose shriek rips through the air as pale light envelops her from her shoulders to her fingertips and on her rear end.

Just like she showed the party in Vulcan's shop, parts of her body have taken on their dragon form.

Stella doesn't intend to hold back whatsoever, even against a low-level goblin.

Skrrring—!

Stella hefts the greatsword in her right dragonized hand—and with alarming quickness. She carried it with ease without her dragon body, but now it looks like she's lifting a twig.

And then—*whoosh*—a thunderous roar resounds. It goes without saying—Stella has brought her greatsword down against the quickly closing goblin. The monster makes to slash at Stella's midsection, but immediately after and with far greater speed, Stella swipes her greatsword. She doesn't move—simply lifts her sword up, then brings it down. That's all she needs to secure her victory.

"Gah-ha-ha! Swords are such fun!"

Stella shrieks again as she looks down at the goblin's corpse, its head split in two with blood and viscera spraying in every direction. As for the spectators...

"Meown, she's strong, but..."

"She might be a bit touched in the head. She's taking far too much pleasure in killing..."

Aria and Vulcan are both a bit creeped out.

Vulcan enjoys being an adventurer to the extent that it lets her collect the materials she needs to create items for her shop. Aria was saved as a child by the Holy Blade—Alisha—and was deeply enamored, making up her mind to be a good-natured, righteous warrior, just like her hero.

Neither of them takes distinct pleasure in killing, by any means. From their perspective, it's impossible to understand Stella's excitement.

She's absolutely murderous... Everything should be fine if she doesn't go down the wrong path, but on the off chance she does...I could be...

Tama realizes as much from witnessing Stella revel in murdering on instinct—she is a monster, after all—but he's also concerned that it will someday come back to bite the party.

If that ever led to his beloved master, Aria, or her partner, Vulcan, being exposed to harm, then...

Of course, Tama intends to provide whatever support and exhaust every means to make sure that doesn't happen.

As for the little behemoth himself, Stella was indeed once his enemy, but now she's his comrade... Well, maybe not quite, but he has begun to think of her more in that regard, to the extent of considering her the object of his protection.

"Unnngh..."

"What's the matter, Stella?"

Stella grumbles unhappily. In response to Aria's query, she replies, "Using a sword is fun, but with enemies this weak, I'll never have a chance to use my shield. I want to go deeper into the labyrinth and fight stronger mid-level enemies!"

"Hmm... Well, with the power you're showing, it will probably be fine to move down to the next level."

"Meown, it might be really tough, but it's true that testing the extent of Stella's true strength could be a good idea."

Setting Stella's personality aside, Aria and Vulcan are indeed after power and profit, so having her battle strength is something to be thankful for.

Putting her through rigorous training to test her strength will allow them to decide what sort of battle style she should settle on as a member of their party.

"Okay, it's decided. Stella, we can see that you're clearly very powerful, but you're fighting for the first time...or at least, you don't remember fighting before, so be on your guard!"

"Gah-ha-ha-ha! No problem! I might not be as strong as you or Tama, but I'm fearsome in my own right, and I have no intention of losing my wits to a bunch of measly monsters!"

Acknowledging Aria's concern, Stella does her boastful best to allay her fears.

The former earth dragon's head is filled with nothing but a desire to go on a full-out rampage.

"Gah-ha-ha-ha-ha! Whaddaya think, Tama? You like my shield-bash skills?"

The final stage of the second level of the labyrinth—

Stella yells with glee as the orc she bashes flies against the far wall, screaming in agony.

She definitely knows how to use a shield... Well, it's more apt to say she knows how to use it one way. Her fighting style is courageous and uninhibited, as expected.

She attacks another orc immediately, a single, fell swoop of her greatsword ripping its head in half. Next, two orcs appear, and Stella exclaims, "Time for my shield!" before tearing into them immediately, eyes livid. The first took a vicious bash full-on and flew across the room.

The second orc stares in bewilderment as its comrade becomes airborne. In that instant, Stella brings down her greatsword again, aiming a powerful blow at the creature's face.

Slash—!

The lethal strike leaves the orc beheaded. Fresh red blood geysers from its neck, and Stella laughs with abandon before leaping forward. She's headed for the orc that has been knocked against the wall. It's obviously taken a direct blow to the face and looks shell-shocked, unable to stand.

"Psh, you can't even summon the power to fight when your enemy stands directly before you... What a bunch of chumps."

Stella spits out her words and lowers her greatsword once more. It goes without saying that the orc's head no longer retains its original shape... By this point, Aria and company have witnessed this brand of battle strategy over and over again.

Tama looks quite nonplussed that Stella hasn't used her shield for defensive purposes even once. Aria and Vulcan remain appalled by her belligerent personality and over-the-top fighting style.

"I know she's a dragonewt, but I really didn't think that Stella would be this powerful."

"Meown, looks like I'm nothing more than a tiger-eared-clan chump, too... I had confidence in my ability, but I can't possibly compete with her."

Aria relies on electric speed in her fighting style, and Vulcan has herculean strength from her feline blood. Both, however, have resigned themselves to Stella's inhuman power. That said, Aria and Vulcan can't help but grin boldly—all while imagining a *certain monster* lurking below them on the third level of the labyrinth.

The third level—

Squelch—squish—squelch.

A grotesque creature makes disgusting noises here, a setting even more bone-chilling than the second.

"Urgh… What on earth is that? It's causing an unspeakable sensation throughout my whole body…!"

Stella looks positively disgusted and furrows her brow, shuddering. She was born in the deep recesses of the labyrinth, and back when she chased Tama, she took a different route to the lower levels. That means she's never seen the monsters that appear on this level and the next.

The creature is called a roper. In the past, Aria was forced into a nasty conflict with them, and they're the monsters that caused her to awaken to her derived skill, Whirlwind Slash.

The writhing tentacles growing from the roper's body are not satisfied with simply stopping the movements of its opponent—if the opponent is female, their tentacles will slide underneath their victim's clothing and sexually defile and impregnate them.

Stella was once a monster, and she can instinctually feel on her skin the danger of this natural predator.

"You there, foul beast! Victory goes to the swift!"

Whoosh—!

As she speaks, Stella begins rushing at the monster. She intends to smash the roper down before it has a chance to grab her.

However—

With a *whoosh*, its writhing tentacles lunge at Stella.

"What the—?!"

The former earth dragon's jaw drops in shock. The roper's tentacles are much more agile than they look. Not to mention, they extend a lot farther than she thought.

Stella had already decided the roper wouldn't be faster or have greater range than she does—hence her abject astonishment.

"Goddammit—!!"

Bwroosh—!

Stella brings her greatsword down in a massive arc toward the encroaching tentacles. She intends to rip through all of them at once with a wide-ranging slash. Her blade isn't exactly razor-sharp, but she is able to gather all the tentacles into a bunch, and her aim is spot-on.

At least, it was for her first attack…

"Bi-giii—!"

Stella decides to go for the roper's body after getting rid of its tentacles. As she quickly closes in, the roper cries out and, in that same moment, sprouts new tentacles. They wriggle and writhe as they erupt from both sides of the monster.

Yes—the roper still had tentacles to spare that it was hiding. They rush past Stella as she moves in quickly, and they attack her.

"Graaaaaah!!" Stella howls. To everyone's surprise, she casts her greatsword and Mega Shield aside as she starts swinging her arms furiously.

"Stella, what are you doing?!"

"This is no good, meow! She's forgotten herself in the face of fear!"

Aria and Vulcan both cry out. They can't just sit by while their party member gets impregnated. The girls rush forward to help Stella.

Amid the fray, a thought crosses Tama's mind as he observes Stella's behavior.

Dammit, Stella! Has this dire situation brought back memories from her past life?!

The way she's swinging her arms—it closely resembles her movements when she attacked Tama during their head-to-head confrontation. In other words, Stella's first battle with a roper has frightened her, and she's now trying to attack as she did when she had a massive body.

This won't end well. Stella has entered dragonewt mode. If my master gets attacked while going in to help her, there will be hell to pay! I have no other choice…

With the cool, calm, and collected thinking of a knight, he's made up his mind.

"Meowrn—!"

Tama growls adorably, and then, from his feet…a number of writhing tentacles the same color as his orange tabby fur appear before his very eyes!

Tama has used one of his skills—Summon Tentacle—that he acquired after eating a roper.

Whoosh—!

Each of the tabby tentacles rushes forward with blinding speed. Some reach for Stella while others stop the roper tentacles that escaped the greatsword.

Tama's remaining tentacles wrap around Aria and Vulcan, gently pulling them back, making sure not to put undue stress on their bodies.

Aria's and Vulcan's eyes go wide in surprise at the appearance of these new tentacles, but once seeing that they're protruding from Tama's feet, they realize it's his skill and stop resisting.

"Meown!" *Aqua Howl!*

As Tama stops all the roper's tentacles and ensures everyone's safety, he unleashes another roar. He's activated his Elemental Howl innate skill, Aqua Howl.

A highly pressurized blast of water breath rips toward the roper—*whoosh*—as it cries out.

Shrrring—!

Aqua Howl pierces the roper in its heart.

"Bi-giiii…"

The creature cries out pathetically and crumples in a heap.

—Hey, Stella, cool your jets!

—*Wh-wha…? Ooh, T-Tama? Mmmph? The tentacle monster is defeated. What happened?*

Stella is still swinging her arms violently as Tama addresses her through telepathy. As expected, she's completely forgotten herself and given in to reckless abandon.

—*If you're talking about the roper, I took care of it. What's with you? Forgetting yourself while up against a low-level monster is not like a dragon at all.*

—*Oof... I'm sorry. It would appear that, in my new form, I'm afraid of monsters that I encounter for the first time. Apparently, my battle with you has left a lasting impression.*

—*......*

Stella answers Tama's question limply. Hearing this, Tama doesn't know what to say. The real reason she flew off the handle stems from...

...the terror she experienced after facing off against Tama, the Fearless Cat, and being slain one month ago.

—*...Don't be timid. That's not something I can say easily, as the one who killed you, but from now on, I will be the one to protect you. That's why I need you to fight the way only you can.*

—*!! Ahhh... Tama, hearing those words from someone I love as dearly as you makes me so happy...! Okay, I got it! I will cast away my fear and fight with all I have!!*

As a man, Tama cannot ignore the fact that he has damaged Stella emotionally. That's why he's made up his mind—assuming his responsibility as a man, from now on, he will protect Stella with every fiber of his being.

Stella silently sheds a tear and responds to him, her smile beaming.

"Tama..."

"Meown—!" *What's the matter, my master?*

Just as Tama and Stella finish their telepathic conversation, Aria calls out to him softly from behind. Tama whirls around to see what's going on and is immediately shocked—Aria's ice-blue eyes have pink hearts floating in them. Her cheeks are flushed red, and she's rubbing her thighs together like she doesn't know what to do with herself.

Aria has gone from elf to full-on nymph mode.

Wh-why?! Just what on earth has aroused my master to this degree?!

Tama simply activated one of his skills to guarantee the safety of everyone in their party—what could have triggered her like this...?

Just as Tama ponders this question—

"Ahhh... Tama, that was quite a skill! Those tentacles were so...dirty! Take those cute little tabby tentacles and just ravage me! ♡"

As she speaks, Aria starts snapping off her bikini armor.

Wh-what the—?! Master, how can you possibly be so stimulated right now?! This is too much! ...Hmm? Hold on—I thought you hated slimy tentacles...?

Last time, Aria was absolutely indignant after her tough battle against the roper that had covered her in sticky white fluid. Tama naturally assumed she hated such nasty creatures...but he was wrong.

Obviously, Aria isn't interested in being sexually assaulted by the disgusting tentacles of a monster as bizarre as a roper. However, if the tentacles belonged to adorable little Tama, she could certainly oblige... More specifically, she wanted them to ravish her.

"Huff...huff... ♡"

"M-meown...?"

Aria is encroaching on Tama, her bikini armor half-stripped-off, and he cries out in confusion as he backs away. The little cat thought this back-and-forth between knight and master would continue endlessly... However...

Tama's chastity is eventually saved by Vulcan, who interferes by saying, "What are you doing, getting turned on in a labyrinth?!"

On the other hand...

"Aha! This must be another playful ritual for conceiving offspring!"

...Stella has been observing the situation, enraptured. This means only one thing—Tama's chastity is now at greater risk than ever before.

"Pi-kiiiii—!"

"Piki-piki—!"

Now that Aria's nymph mode has subsided, the party of four begins treading farther into the deep recesses of the third level of the labyrinth.

Ropers appear in front of the adventurers—two this time—and just like the one earlier, they cry out excitedly when they see the three gorgeous females.

"Hmph, more indecent, foul beasts? I messed up before, but not this time!"

—That's the spirit, Stella! I'm here to support you, so give it all you got!

Tama sends a telepathic message of encouragement as Stella shouts her intention to go hard on the ropers. Her cheeks flush red for a moment before she kicks off the ground—*whoosh*—and flies toward them.

Sllllsppp—!

The ropers' tentacles rush quickly for her. Just as before, they intend to capture Stella and impregnate her. But this time, she doesn't hesitate. She doesn't have to because the security provided by the Fearsome Cat—Tama—protecting her has completely eased her fears.

Tama is already on the move, too. Just as Stella rushed forward, he already sprang in front of Aria and Vulcan.

Realizing that Tama intends to go out for support, Vulcan stays put. Aria does the same, but...her cheeks are flushed pink, and her breathing is quite ragged. She's likely thinking, *Oh—ohhh... I get to see Tama's tentacles in action again!* ♡

Tama is watching her reaction and already knows that if he uses his tentacle skill, the elf girl will devolve even further into a nymph. He settles on using a different skill to support Stella.

"Meown—!"

Tama lets out a piercing yet adorable mew. At the same time, he reaches up with his right front paw and swipes it down.

Shrrring—!

The shrill sound that follows is accompanied by the roper's screams.

"*Pi-gyaaaaaa—?!*"

The roper's tentacles that had been reaching for Stella are ripped to shreds as they fly across the room.

"M-meow? What was that?"

"Tama...were you still hiding another skill from us?"

The spectacle has Aria and Vulcan absolutely dumbfounded.

Tama used an absorbed skill that he acquired one month ago—Dragon Claw—to create a massive claw formed by mana that ripped through the roper's tentacles. The fact that he missed Stella as she rushed forward, cutting through only his targets, is a testament to his high degree of skill.

"*Pi-ki—?!*"

The second roper had also been outstretching its tentacles, but seeing its comrade's appendages obliterated, it stops dead in its tracks.

Now!

Spotting this, Stella races forward even faster and lays into the dazed roper with its tentacles cut off for a vicious shield-bash attack. As it recoils from the impact, it spurts milky white fluid, which lands all over Stella's face like a bukkake scene. Despite the not-so-glamorous situation, Stella appears unbothered.

She's also covered in blood, and if anything, she's excited by it as she smiles triumphantly and turns to the other roper, ramming her greatsword directly into its heart. The presence of the blood of her enemies on her skin only ignites her thirst for battle, something that must be part of Stella's nature as a former dragon.

Aria pushes a towel toward Stella, whose body is covered in sticky white fluid, as she asks, "Stella, how does it feel fighting alongside Tama?"

Stella has a look of pure exhilaration on her face as she replies, "It's invigorating! This is my first time fighting with someone else backing me up—I didn't think it would be this incredible!"

Seeing Stella panting as she wipes the white liquid from her face, her cheeks flushed red from battle, is, well... Actually, let's just stop there.

Moving right along—for Stella, who formerly reigned as the undisputed superior being of the entire labyrinth, fighting along-side another party member is an entirely new feeling.

What's more, her partner was Tama, a male she's attracted to, so maybe it makes sense that she's this excited.

"That's called teamwork, you hear me, meow? Stella, you're going to keep fighting by our side and help us make the most pow-erful team possible!"

"Ohhh! I'll be fighting alongside you guys, too, not just Tama? I can't wait!"

"Hee-hee, I'm glad you're so up-front about everything. I think we'll make a great team, right, Vulcan?"

"Meown—!! With the dragonewt Stella in our crew, nothing can stop us now!"

Hearing that she can also fight with Aria and Vulcan, Stella looks even more thrilled than before. She's discovered the sense of joy that accompanies fighting beside her comrades.

Seeing this, Aria and Vulcan are relieved, knowing that, with Stella in their party, their battles will now greatly expand in scope. Their hearts are filled to the brim with hope.

Just then...

Hmm... Well, I sure hope it all goes according to plan...

Tama alone seems concerned. Stella may look innocent, but she is a former monster. Everything will be fine if Tama supports her, but if they start working in tandem...that's what has him worried.

And those worries will become reality sooner than he thinks.

"Stella, you have incredible strength as a dragonewt and carry a massive defensive armament, your Mega Shield, so we want you to become a tank, okay meow?"

"*'Tank'*? Just what does that mean?"

"It's the cornerstone of the party—they stand in the vanguard and draw in enemy attacks. Because you have a greatsword, it would be ideal if you could both take the offensive—as an attacker—and protect the party as a tank..."

Now that Stella understands the joy of fighting alongside comrades, Vulcan begins telling her about different battle positions.

Stella wonders, *A tank? Is it delicious?* as Aria explains a tank's role to her. Just then—

"Gah-ha-ha-ha-ha! If that's what you mean, then leave it to me! In other words, I just need to be at the front of the party and go wild, right? Perfect!"

Excited by the prospect of fighting on the front line, Stella laughs with abandon. She looks ready to take on any monster, roper or otherwise.

"Meown—! That's so great to hear right meow!"

"We didn't have a tank until now, so it's a huge help that you've joined our party!"

Vulcan and Aria express their appreciation in lively, joyous voices. Before, Vulcan, Aria, and Tama were all on the offensive as attackers, and they didn't have a tank. Of course, Tama can activate Divine Lion Protection or Iron Body if he chooses, and making use of his orichalcum armor, he can become a tank in a sense, but Aria and Vulcan don't know this.

Under these circumstances, having Stella join as a dragonewt (at least they think she is) shield-wielder is very meaningful. Vulcan will be able to brandish her battle hammer without really having to worry about enemy attacks, and Aria will be free to dart around with her knives to her heart's content and easily perform sneak attacks. Tama, too, having been an all-around supporter of the party thus far, will be able to adapt to the situation at hand like never before.

"Okay then, let's move forward with Stella at the helm... Hee-hee, look at that! Some new enemies have appeared. Perfect timing!"

Just as she begins to speak, Aria laughs fearlessly and fixes her gaze forward.

From the dimly lit corridor ahead of the party—

"Bu-hiii..."

New monsters appear in time with a guttural growl. It's obvious from the sound—they're pig-faced orcs, five of them. Meeting this many orcs at once on this level of the labyrinth is rare, but the timing couldn't be better. It's a perfect chance to test how easy the fight will be with Stella, their attacker and tank specialist, now among their ranks.

"Gah-ha-ha-ha! Come at me, pigs!"

Stella creeps closer to the orcs and bashes her greatsword and Mega Shield together loudly. The obsidian steel blade and shield cause a piercing crash, and the orcs that were previously looking at either Aria, Vulcan, or Stella (perhaps each had its favorite) all turn to Stella.

"Bu-hiiiii—!"

"Oink! Oink!"

The five orcs descend on her at once, their eyes tinged bloodred. They seem enraged at having been called "pigs."

Two of the orcs have stone axes while the other three are barehanded. The first in line raises its stone ax to swing it down on Stella.

Orcs are massive. Taking a single blow from their stone weapons wielded with such formidable power would spell the end of anyone... Or so they think—

"Hmph. That's all you got, pig?!"

Stella reacts calmly and deflects the orc's blow with her Mega Shield. The orc's ax and her shield slam together with a thunderous clash, but she doesn't budge an inch. After all, she is a dragon, if only part of her.

"Now it's my turn!"

Seeing how deflecting its blow was a piece of cake for Stella, the orc's eyes bug out of its face.

For the newly minted tank, this is too easy. She's already raised her greatsword high in the air and swiftly drops it on the orc.

"Bu-byaaaaaaa—!"

The beast emits a bloodcurdling scream, and in the same moment, fresh blood sprays through the air, streaming from the orc's shoulder.

Thanks to Stella's greatsword, the orc's arm has been sliced—no, lopped right off its body.

Normally, she should have been able to cleave through the orc's shoulder all the way through to its heart, but she held back while maintaining a defensive position. This caused her power to plummet and only rip off the enemy's arm.

The orc, who could have simply perished in a single moment, is now dealing with unbearable, hellish pain and is lost in a world of misery.

"Bu-gi...iii...!"

The monster contorts its face in agony from the searing pain in its shoulder and cries out.

Seeing Stella's ferocious capacity for incomparable destruction, the four orcs in their fellow's wake all stop dead in their tracks. Just then—

"Bu-hiiiii—!"

The lot of them screech again in unison, and in the same moment, the orc that lost its arm turns on a dime with alarming speed, like a rabbit escaping a predator, and runs away.

"Wha—?! You dare flee from your enemy?! You impudent monster scum! Halt!"

Stella rushes after the fugitive and separates from the party.

"Stella! You must not abandon your position!"

"Yeah, leave the enemy that escaped alone for meow!"

Aria and Vulcan yell after Stella as she moves away from them, but as a former monster, Stella has activated her hunter's instinct and doesn't hear them pleading for her to stop.

She disappears into the darkness of the labyrinth and out of sight.

Goddamn Stella! I knew this was coming!

Tama had a feeling that something like this would happen and curses Stella. He simultaneously gives a soft "meow!" and is subsequently enveloped in a golden light along with Aria and Vulcan. He's activated his buff skill, Divine Lion Protection.

"Bu-hi-hihihi—!"

Immediately thereafter, the remaining orcs smile sickeningly and stare down Aria, Vulcan, and Tama. Now that their powerful foe, Stella, has disappeared, they're convinced they'll be able to defile this trio with ease.

"Oh well, meow, what can ya do? We'll have to clean them up ourselves!"

"Got it, Vulcan! Tama, if it gets rough, please lend us your support!"

"Meown—!" *Leave it to me, master!*

Four orcs… Normally, this would be quite the bitter battle, but with the benefit of Divine Lion Protection surrounding them, it should be a cinch…or at the very least, a lopsided battle that they'll surely come out of on top.

Aria and company already know this, which is why they decide to stick around and take care of the rest of the orcs. They don't even really need conviction. Tama can just wipe them out with an Elemental Howl, but the party is treating the battle as a training exercise—current unforeseen circumstances notwithstanding.

They'll certainly aim for their best performance, given the situation. Neither Aria nor Vulcan wants to win too easily. That's why Aria gave Tama the order to stand down unless necessary.

"Let's go meow!"

As the orcs charge them with bloodcurdling battle cries, Vulcan lifts her battle hammer high into the air and attacks. When she hefts the hammer, she does it with a sense of levity not seen thus far. And rightly so—she's imbued with Tama's Divine Lion Protection. One of its effects is the blessing of additional strength.

Vulcan drops her battle hammer with incredible speed. The orc she's aiming for doesn't even have a chance to react in surprise—its skull is crushed from above with a thunderous smack.

"Bu-gi-gyaaaaaa—?!"

One of the other orcs cries out from the rear. In front of it stands Aria in quiet repose with her blade in hand. Her knife is sunk to its hilt into the orc's eyeball.

Thanks to the boost to her speed from her skill, Acceleration, combined with Divine Lion Protection, she has acquired literal "god speed" to support her already skilled movements. She rushes out from behind Vulcan, but the orc is unable to respond before she gouges its eyeball.

The monster's body immediately crumples faceup in a thunderous heap on the ground. Aria's single attack has pierced its brain.

Fwhoosh—!

After bringing down her target, Aria quickly retreats to the rear guard as the last remaining orc swings its stone ax at her. It whiffs through the air.

The massive momentum of that whiff pulls the orc off-balance and—*crrrack*—!

A sharp *thwack* signals Vulcan's battle hammer smashing into the orc's flank. From the sound, she's easily crushed a number of its ribs.

As she retracts her hammer, Vulcan yells, "Aria!"

Aria is already in a crouching start and rushes forward immediately at the call.

Lightning speed—Aria closes the distance between herself and the orc in no time flat.

She brings both knives across the orc's neck and cuts through like butter, leaving it decapitated. She's able to pull off this feat thanks to her speed combined with the *tamahagane*-and-orichalcum alloy from which her knives are forged.

"Ugh, Stella, I told you not to leave your post!"

Having finished off the last orc, Aria yells into the depths of the labyrinth.

Just like that, Stella is back.

Judging from the blood in which she's covered, she's dealt with the orc that tried to run away.

"Why? Why must I act like my prey can simply escape?"

Stella stares blankly at Aria. For her, defeating a monster is the same as killing prey.

Furthermore, Stella mistakenly believes that Aria and Vulcan are the most fearsome warriors around. For that reason, it didn't even occur to her that running off would cause a problem.

"We were okay this time, but if the monsters we were facing had been a higher level, we could have been in trouble, meow! So don't just go rogue on us— Wait, where are you going—?!"

Just as Vulcan starts another lecture on the importance of teamwork, Stella has already dashed away and gone rogue again. Gazing far ahead of them, Aria and Vulcan can see another orc in the distance.

Hmph... Just how are we going to rein in that reckless tomboy...?

Tama has his doubts about Stella.

"Huff..."

"I'm s-so beat..."

Aria and Vulcan sigh heavily near the entrance to the labyrinth. Their shoulders droop, and they are absolutely exhausted.

Understandably so.

When Stella ran off again earlier, Aria and Vulcan chased her and pleaded for her to be more careful, but it was no use. Thanks to their newest member throwing their party out of order, both Vulcan and Aria nearly fell prey to roper tentacles and the miserable fate of being covered by their milky white ooze.

They also nearly got surrounded by multiple orcs, and in one instance, they were almost cornered in an ambush. Both times, Tama used his cleverness to activate his skills Summon Tentacle and Elemental Howl to successfully defeat their enemies and persevere.

Had they proceeded to a more dangerous level, they might not have been so lucky. With that in mind, the party agreed to turn back for today.

Due to the untenable battle situations into which they'd been thrown and general fatigue, they had to abandon most of the materials they'd gathered in the labyrinth. They'll barely make any earnings today.

"Hmph… I still didn't get it out of my system…"

In comparison to Aria and company's apparent exhaustion, Stella doesn't appear the least bit tired, despite having run around the labyrinth to her heart's content. If anything, she still wants to fight more and looks dissatisfied.

"Phew… Finally, we're back outside. Come here, Tama!"

"Meown—!"

Having stepped out of the caverns into the sunshine, Aria turns toward Tama with outstretched arms. She intends to carry him home in her bosom.

Tama mews enthusiastically in response and hops up to her healthy twin peaks. He makes sure to not harm them as he leaps.

"Ahhh—holding you really lifts my spirits, Tama. Thank you for protecting us so much today. ♡"

"Meown?"

As Tama dives between Aria's breasts, her expression melts. She brings her lips softly to Tama's forehead and kisses him to express her thanks for today. Tama mews in surprise from the sudden display of affection and rubs his head lovingly against Aria's cheek.

"Hee-hee, Tama, that tickles!"

Even though she claims it's ticklish, Aria also rubs her cheek against Tama. Seeing this, Vulcan whines, "Meow, I'm so jealous of you right meow, Aria!"

As the three of them interact...

—Hey, Tama! I want to hold you, too!

Stella's telepathic voice reverberates through Tama's head—he already knew it was her.

—I refuse. I only allow those to whom my master gives permission to hold me. If you still really want to, you must receive her blessing.

Tama responds coldly. Just as he said, he's never been held by anyone unless by Aria's leave. Not to mention, Stella caused them all so much trouble today. His icy reply was intended to let her know that she should repent.

"Hey, Aria. It's my turn to hold Tama now."

"...? I'm afraid I must decline, Stella. Tama is my knight. I will not so easily hand him over to someone who intends to rob him of his chastity!"

"Whaaa...?! But, my lady...!!"

Aria is perplexed by this sudden change in address, but no matter what Stella calls her, Aria simply denies her request. Stella is visibly flabbergasted. She always thought that Aria was a kind and gentle master and didn't seriously consider the elf would deny her the chance to hold Tama.

Aria is a kind and gentle girl, no doubt. Under normal

circumstances, she generally lets others hold Tama. However, like she said, Stella intends to deflower her pet…

In other words, she's a threat. Stella is a high-level beauty with the allure of a grown woman.

This means that Tama, who Aria loves dearly, has not been lured in by Stella's scent.

"Tama is…the Fearsome Cat! As a weakling, you aren't a proper match for him!"

"Wha…?! What are you trying to say, Stella?"

Suddenly, Aria's demeanor shifts from staid to downright indignant. She is shocked by Stella's claim that she isn't the right girl for Tama!

What shift has occurred in Stella's heart…making her say something to ruffle Aria's feathers like that?

"I understand after today's battles! You are so much weaker than I thought. Tama should not be serving an orcish woman like you who's always lagging behind!"

Ohhh, is that what she means…?

Vulcan has formed a hypothesis: Stella has been following Aria's orders because she treats Tama, the all Fearsome Cat, like a child. In other words, she's upset because she'd assumed that Aria was even more powerful than Tama.

This is also why she looked so terrified of Aria the first time they met.

"Tama, come here to my bosom! Together we shall beget a child of fearsome strength!"

Saying this, Stella rushes toward Tama ensconced in Aria's bosom and… *Squish—!* Her breasts aren't as big as Aria's but they're still ripe and soft as they push against Tama.

"Meowr—?!" *Eep?!*

Tama cries out in fear as Aria and Stella squeeze him between their massive mammaries. It's all happened so fast; Tama gives in to his behemoth-cub instincts and buries his face deeper into Aria's bosom.

"Ha-ha! ♪ Did you see that, Stella? Tama loves my breasts! You can try to seduce him all you want—it won't work!"

"Grrrr…! Tama, does Aria really make you that happy?! In that case, I will draw your gaze to me by force!"

It's true that, as far as battle is concerned, Aria is still inexperienced in many ways. But that doesn't matter. She loves Tama with every fiber of her being, and Tama has promised her his undying loyalty.

Aria smiles coyly, provoking Stella even further. The former earth dragon glares back angrily, her face contorted with fury and frustration. Sparks erupt between their fiery gazes.

Still squished between the two girls' velvety soft breasts, Tama trembles with fear at the thought of what will become of him.

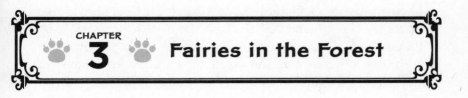
Squish, squeeze! Jiggle, bounce!

Ahhh... Being stuck between my master's breasts is as wonderful and calming as ever...

On the way home from the labyrinth—today, just as any other day, Tama is tucked snugly in Aria's cleavage, which bounces with each step she takes. The soft vibrations put the little kitten completely at ease.

"Meown—! How cute! Tama looks so beyond relaxed right meow!"

Vulcan can feel the motherly love flowing from Aria's warmth and softness, and seeing Tama's expression, her heart skips a beat.

"Grrr...! Someday, I'll be the one to make Tama that happy!"

Next to Vulcan, Stella—who lost to Aria in the first battle for Tama's affection—looks positively dejected as she spits out her words. At this point, she doesn't just want Tama's seed. She now craves being able to dote on him, just like Aria does.

However, Aria can't even hear her rival right now. She's absorbed in Tama loving on her and looking completely safe and secure. Before she realizes it, the party has arrived at the Adventurers Guild located in the city center.

They were able to collect materials from only a small number of monsters, but they will still earn some cash today. They need to take what they can get—and they also have two more reasons to stop by the guild.

The first is to show Stella how materials collected from monsters can be sold—a chance to teach her how money is made.

The second is to properly register her as an adventurer. She intends to continue working in this profession moving forward, and most importantly, her adventurer's tag will act as her identification.

Stella has lost her memories (at least that's what everyone thinks), so the tag will be very useful as she comes into her own.

Aria opens the door to the guild. It's early evening, and the place is packed with people—in front of the noticeboard, at the registration counter, around the meeting tables, and in the bar.

The adventurers clamoring at the noticeboard are choosing quests of their liking for tomorrow. Avid adventurers can't afford to lose a moment preparing for the next day.

Others who have just received their pay dash directly to the bar in the back to wash down salty snacks with a cold ale.

As usual, several drunk adventurers are making passes at a guild staff member busing dishes, pulling her toward them.

"Wow! So this is an adventurers guild!"

An excited voice cuts through the chaos—it's Stella, standing next to Aria.

Labyrinthos is a city bustling with activity, but the interior of the guild is positively teeming with life.

Stella appears excited by everything around her—her eyes are lit up like a Christmas tree.

"Yo, lookit that chick! She's a total babe!"

"Maybe she's new? Check out that body and outfit—she's showing under boob and her ass is half-out... Drives me crazy!"

Stella's boisterous exclamation draws the collective gaze of the adventurers. The men are instantly transfixed by her gorgeous looks and cry out in amazement at her provocative outfit.

Stella has a perfect face; two perfectly ripe, bouncy breasts; a pert, juicy round ass; and tight lines running down her abs. She's covered by a thin piece of fabric across her chest and wearing hot pants that show the top of her butt... The men reacting like this is really no surprise.

"Hold up, she's hot, too, but look at Aria! She's wearing bikini armor...! Her old adventuring outfit was great, but this shows off her cleavage to the max...!"

"Side boob is definitely even more salacious than Aria's cleavage! I'm team Vulcan for life."

A single adventurer's comment has brought all eyes in the guild to Aria and Vulcan. Just as they claimed, Aria now wears bikini armor that is even more highly revealing than her previous ensemble. Of course this brings focus to the deep valley between her melon peaks.

As an added bonus, the gorgeous porcelain skin of her waist, back, and thighs is also fully exposed. Plus, the bottom of the bikini is so tiny, the men can barely believe it—what's known as "low-rise."

Of course, this allows for Aria's perfect hip lines and plump thighs to be fully admired.

Lastly, Vulcan isn't showing quite as much skin as Stella or Aria. That said, her outfit consists of a pair of overalls with nothing underneath. Her healthy, straw-colored armpits and perfectly ripe breasts visible from the side of her overalls will dig deeply into the perverted mind of any man.

All three of the girls are quite frankly bombshells with amazing bodies, so much so that a number of the men staring are holding their crotches and bent forward, unable to move.

"Hmm? It seems these human males are staring at me. And their gazes are rather unpleasant."

"Ugh... I feel like we're getting even more stares than before..."

"Meown, what can you do? Stella's joined us now, and you're wearing a new outfit..."

Seeing the men's reactions, Stella looks upset, as if she knows instinctively that they're all staring at her licentiously.

Aria, who dislikes human males, is similarly taken aback. Her expression is tense as she unconsciously clutches Tama to her chest even tighter.

Vulcan already knew this would happen, and her speech reflects this as her tiger-clan ears fold down—she's already given up.

At just that moment—

"Rrrroooowwwwlll—!!"

""""What the—?!""""

Tama bristles while ensconced in Aria's bosom and growls in fierce intimidation toward the adventurers and their vulgar gazes.

Tama looks cute and cuddly, but he's an S-ranked monster, after all. The power latent in his body—not to mention his aggression—is beyond exceptional. The adventurers in the guild are getting just a glimpse of his fearsome power.

They also now understand that anyone who brings harm Aria's way will not be forgiven…

Hmm. That should do it. I will not excuse any brute who casts a filthy glance my master's way.

Seeing the men quaking in their boots, Tama gives a satisfied "Meown!"

"Hee-hee, Tama, thank you so much."

"Meown—Tama, you are such a good boy."

"Incredible! A single cry from his mouth…! My future husband is so cool!"

Responding to Tama's actions, Aria, Vulcan, and Stella all praise him gleefully.

Stella was a dragon in her past life, so if she wants to, she can be just as formidable as Tama…but never mind that.

Just as Aria nuzzles her cheek against Tama for saving them from the men's licentious gazes, she hears someone say, "Hey now, if it isn't Aria and company. And…is this a new friend of yours?"

In the same moment, the male adventurers' faces all freeze in even further shock. It's a reasonable response. The voice is accompanied by a six-foot-tall, muscle-bound, bald-headed, strapping beast of a man (or lady?) in full bondage gear.

Affectionately known as Anna, Arnold Holzweilzenegger—this guild's receptionist girl (???)—has appeared.

"Hello, Anna! Yes, this is Stella, and starting today, she's beginning life as an adventurer with us!"

"Anna, we'd like to register Stella, okay meow?"

Aria's and Vulcan's smiles widen when they see Arnold. This is because Aria has always stuck by Anna's side like a sister, and Vulcan knows how great of a person Arnold is.

"Before that, Aria, I have something to tell you—is now a good time?"

"...? What could that be?"

Arnold has something to share that eclipses Stella's introduction or registration as an adventurer. Aria is endlessly curious and has a puzzled look on her face.

"Please allow me to explain."

Who now? A voice can be heard from behind Arnold, where a man stands.

"It's a pleasure to meet you, Aria. My name is Leis. I have a special mission for you, which is why I'm here today."

The man named Leis steps out from Arnold's shadow. He looks to be in his mid-forties. White strands streak through his brown hair, and a number of wrinkles have worn themselves underneath his eyes.

Leis is of average height and average build, and he's wearing an expensive suit with an overcoat. He likely holds some high status or is quite wealthy.

However, rather than noticing his clothing, Aria is focused on something about his eyes. His pupils are gray and sorrowful...or perhaps some form of mistrust is growing within Aria.

The intuition of an elf who grew up in the wild is sharp as a

razor. It's often said they can tell if someone has ill intentions the moment they meet.

What is this? He doesn't seem to be a bad person...but...

Aria senses something off about Leis...but she can't determine its exact nature.

Just then—

"A special-mission request just for you, oh mew god! It appears word is getting out about your strength, Aria!"

Hearing that Leis has a special mission just for Aria, Vulcan is elated, as if Leis was talking about her. A special-mission request is definitive proof of prowess and name value. Because Vulcan trained Aria, she's ecstatic that her pupil is now getting recognition.

Hearing how happy Vulcan is, Aria decides to quell her misgivings and first asks Leis, "A special-mission request... Just what sort of errand does this entail? And why are you asking me? There are far more experienced adventurers here in the guild..."

"The mission is an escort quest. I am a merchant and transporting a *certain item* from the town of Renald to the earl's territory, Gladstone, and I require protection for myself and my cargo."

"They requested you specially because I referred you, Aria! ♪ You succeeded in driving out the demons from Renald with Vulcan, and you have Tama, who can take down four trolls all by himself, right? Above all else, Leis has requested someone he can trust explicitly, which is why I thought of you and your strong sense of justice. ♪"

Leis and Arnold answer Aria's questions in turn.

Huh... They've asked for Aria by name—not me—due to her strength and trustworthiness...

Hearing the two speak, Tama nods slightly in distinct agreement. Vulcan is equally happy, seeing so much trust being placed in Aria, who was just a D-ranked adventurer when the two met.

"Well, we can only do so much standing here—shall we have a seat, and I'll explain the matter in detail? Actually, I have something I'd like to ask of Vulcan, also..."

"Meown? Something for me, too? I'm sorry, but right meow, I can't leave my shop unattended for an extended period. I'm afraid I'll have to refuse in this meow-ment."

"Is that so…? I understand. What a pity."

Leis had intended to ask Vulcan, from Aria's same party, to undertake a different special mission, it seems. However, she's tasked with the responsibility of running her shop.

The trip from Renald to Gladstone is over three days by horse-drawn carriage. Thinking of the round-trip journey, Vulcan had no choice but to refuse.

"Okay then, please provide further details. Stella…should probably not be present, judging by her appearance. Vulcan, can you please go ahead and get her something to eat?"

"Okay meow!"

Aria originally thought to encourage Stella, the other member of their party, to listen as well, but seeing the look on her face, she gave up. A whiff of the tantalizing aroma wafting from the bar at the back of the guild has Stella lost in a trance, drool streaming from her mouth.

Vulcan leads their drooling companion away while Aria, still holding Tama, sits to continue her conversation with Leis and Arnold.

"Okay then, let's explain. As Leis said earlier, what we want you to do, Aria, is guard a convoy. The items requiring your diligence are Leis himself and his cargo, the skeleton of an earth dragon."

"An earth dragon skeleton…! And from the town of Renald…"

"That's right. About a month ago, an earth dragon corpse appeared, and the skeleton was harvested from it. Right, Tama?"

Responding to Aria's surprise, Arnold affirms her suspicions. The *"certain item"* they'll be transporting is the earth dragon Tama destroyed in the labyrinth approximately one month earlier in order to save his master—in other words, Stella's skeleton.

The sudden appearance of an earth dragon corpse coincident with Tama's battle wounds had sent rumors spreading far and wide.

The stories are circulating, and it's clear that Arnold, who shoots a wink Tama's way, already knows them. The little cat, however, merely cocks his head to the side as if to say, *What are you on about?*

Aria asks how exactly Leis came into possession of the earth dragon skeleton, and he replies, "Actually, there was an auction for the corpse in Renald. I bid on the skeleton only, because it can be used in trading."

As a merchant, perhaps Leis intends to sell the skeleton as raw materials to a blacksmith, or maybe he has a different use for it in mind...

Aria is definitely curious but declines to pry further. Her intuition as an elf is telling her that Leis doesn't have ulterior motives, and above all else, she trusts Arnold. He always takes thorough measures and strictly vets the requestor, to make sure he passes on only legitimate requests.

"I would like to leave as early as possible. Tomorrow, if feasible... How does this amount strike you for payment?"

Leis answers Aria's questions while detailing the conditions of his request, pushing an official form from the guild toward Aria.

"...Th-this price... You can't be serious...?"

"I am very serious; my cargo is extremely precious."

The quote on the request form is staggering, vastly eclipsing the estimate for the quest Aria had accepted previously, the one that led to the defeat of the demon Beryl.

"Yes, and there's a chance the earth dragon skeleton will be preyed on by thieves. That's why the fee is quite high. There's a certain level of danger involved, but you and Tama can handle it, I'm sure. ♪"

"...In that case, I believe I would like to accept this quest. Tama, you're okay with it, right?"

"Meown—!" *Of course, master!*

Aria has made up her mind and accepted the mission. Tama, lying quietly on the table, enthusiastically affirms her decision.

"By the way, can she...can Stella come along with us, too?"

"If she's your comrade, then of course she can. The more bodies the better for a convoy."

Aria can't afford to leave Stella alone in Labyrinthos and is relieved when Leis readily and affably consents to having her accompany them.

Fighting a number of monsters in a confined space like the labyrinth is one thing, but along the route they'll be traveling, Stella can't be expected to cooperate quite as closely. If she runs off on her own, it will be slightly more tolerable.

Also, Aria is confident this will be a good chance for Stella to get used to fighting while defending a specific item.

Hmm... Will this work out? If Stella is joining us, that means she'll see the earth dragon skeleton—her corpse from her previous life. She could be scarred beyond repair...

Hearing that Stella will join them, Tama can't help but imagine the possibility. His old enemy is now a comrade joining him on the front lines of battle.

Tama turns to see the former earth dragon tearing into her food playfully with Vulcan by her side. The former knight inevitably fears for the girl's state of mind.

"This is incredible... It's really just the bones, isn't it?"

"Yes, the dissection was performed by professionals who removed the skeleton. It remains in pristine condition."

Two days later, Aria and company have reached the town of Renald.

Aria and the requestor, Leis, are discussing the earth dragon skeleton—Stella's corpse from her past life.

"..."

—Stella, are you okay...?

Tama gingerly engages Stella in telepathic conversation as she stands next to Aria and Leis, looking up at her remains silently.

Last night, Tama told Stella that the object they'd be protecting on this quest is her past self's corpse. As expected, she was deeply scarred by this revelation. She currently seems very dejected.

She used to be able to eat mountains of food, but now her appetite is only as much as a normal human's.

Seeing Stella's sudden change in mood, Aria thought she should leave her behind with Vulcan, but Stella put up a fuss, claiming she *"doesn't want to be separated from Tama…,"* so they brought her along.

The party was attacked by a number of monsters on the way to Renald, but Stella refused to help fight them off. Tama cleaned them all up with Elemental Howls.

—*Tama…*

—*What is it, Stella?*

—*It's so strange… When I saw my corpse, I remembered the moment you took my life…and for some reason, it made my lady parts throb!*

—*……*

Tama is left completely speechless.

"By the way, Leis, how are we expected to transport this massive skeleton? I don't think that horses will be of any use…"

"You don't need to worry about that, Aria. I have six carrier lizards pulling a specially made orichalcum-alloy carriage. It will hold under the weight."

"I see. Then I guess we don't have anything to worry about!"

Carrier lizards are a particularly rare species, about seven feet long. They are as intelligent as horses and have strong, powerful bodies—the perfect creature to carry heavy cargo a long distance.

"Hey now, if it isn't Aria and Tama!"

As they converse, Aria and Leis hear a voice call out to them.

"Mr. Town Headman! It's so nice to see you again!"

"Meown—!"

The town headman, who submitted the request that resulted in the death of the demon Beryl, appears before them, grinning from ear to ear. Of course he is—Aria and Tama are the heroes who saved the town of Renald.

"I'm so glad to see both of you are well again! Are you the adventurers I heard will be protecting this earth-dragon-skeleton cargo?"

"Yes, that's correct. We received a special request from this man, Leis..."

"Wooow, isn't that something! And it seems that your adventurer rank has gone up, too. Maybe that's a given for someone who's defeated a demon?"

The headman looks toward Aria's chest while he speaks. Just as he claimed, her adventurer's tag has changed from silver to gold—in other words, she's increased from C to B rank.

Though Vulcan's cooperation always helps, her prowess in taking down the demon and Tama's record of defeating four trolls by himself was recognized, and she was promoted just as they left on their journey. Of course, that means that Vulcan also rose to B rank.

Grrr. Damn headman, pretending to look at Aria's adventurer's tag while he stares at her resplendent valley. It's time to teach you a lesson.

Realizing that the headman is leering, Tama jumps up from the ground onto Aria's chest and burrows in between her breasts before turning to the headman and narrowing his adorable little eyes.

No matter how cute he might look, Tama is a powerful elemental cat that can take down multiple A-rank monsters single-handedly.

The headman yelps in fright and quickly averts his eyes.

Attempting to change the subject, the he looks toward Stella and says to Aria, "W-well, let's forget about that for now... Who is that girl over there, breathing so raggedly...?"

Stella's cheeks are visibly red, and she's panting excitedly.

This foul creature! Is she recalling the moment I put her to death and getting all hot and bothered by it?!

Tama had been devoting all his strength to protecting Aria from the headman's wandering gaze, but seeing Aria's current condition, his eyes go wide as saucers in surprise.

No matter what the circumstances, getting turned on from recalling the moment of one's death is simply more than Tama can comprehend.

Well...in reality, Stella isn't getting excited by the fact that Tama killed her but rather recalling his strength once again and wondering, *What would happen if Tama had his way with me in that behemoth form...? I'll bet one shot would be all it would take to impregnate me...*

That much was beyond the scope of Tama's imagination.

Well, I guess that's that; no matter what shape or form it takes, she's clearly overcome her trauma. This means she should get her appetite back, and she'll be able to return to battle.

Tama forces himself to believe it's all true.

The town headman invites Aria and the party to stay a night at Renald's inn. They accept, including a delicious meal and an open-air hot bath to relieve and soothe the fatigue of their travels, preparing them for tomorrow's journey.

"By the way, can I ask you something?"

"What is it, Aria? Provided I'm able, I'm happy to answer any questions you might have."

Leis responds to Aria's query with a cheerful smile. Their journey has been pleasant thus far. A few monsters, including goblins, attacked them, but because they're on convoy protection duty, Aria and company stayed in the back and allowed Tama to clear the path with Elemental Howls, just like on their journey to Renald.

They've proceeded along their route and have currently entered their second evening. The group dines together as the campfire crackles.

According to their itinerary, if they leave early tomorrow morning, they should arrive at their destination of Gladstone just before noon.

Meanwhile, Aria continues with her question.

"What sort of merchant trade will the earth dragon skeleton be used for? The auction price you told me makes it seem like it's not really that profitable..."

Adventurers generally do not ask those requesting their assistance such deep questions. However, over the past two days, Aria has come to realize that Leis is a kind man with a good heart. Given this fact, she made up her mind that getting a little curious and asking a few questions couldn't hurt.

"That's a good question... Between you and me, I have an arms dealer merchant friend who has wanted an earth dragon skeleton for quite some time. He had a premonition of a massive war that is soon to come..."

"Is that so? Well, I better not pry any deeper for details, in that case..."

Aria is convinced by Leis's story.

A massive war... Will it be a struggle over territory by the aristocracy, or will two nations collide suddenly? Large mercantile families are often well-informed when it comes to such matters, and the information is kept strictly confidential.

Leis has divulged this insight to Aria, although it is ambiguous. For the elf, however, that is more than enough.

If a huge war starts, so many innocent lives will be lost...

Imagining the horror, Aria casts her gaze downward. It's easy for her to fight in the name of righteousness when her opponents are demons and monsters, but against another human, it's nearly impossible.

Aria feels lost, and this immovable truth rankles her sense of righteousness.

"Meown..."

"Hee-hee, Tama, are you consoling me? You are such a sweetheart."

Tama's cheeks are stuffed with grilled meat, but he hops onto Aria's lap and rubs his head lovingly into her stomach.

Aria smiles faintly and strokes Tama's head with tender love and care.

"Grrrrr... Just what do you love so much about this weak little girl?"

Stella hasn't had another chance to hold Tama since the first time. This is because Aria hasn't let her guard down around Stella, who is prowling after Tama's manhood.

"I'm more interested in how gorgeous girls like you and Stella became adventurers. It's mysterious. With looks like those, you must have a multitude of high-level adventurers and aristocrats lining up to take your hand..."

With a smirk in Stella's direction, Leis compliments her and Aria while expressing his fascination that they make their living as adventurers despite their obvious beauty.

In response, Aria says, "You're right. I have been pursued by an aristocrat before. However, I am not fond of human men. And I need to get stronger, to save as many people as possible. That's why I'm training to be an adventurer."

Recalling how Kussman pursued her, Aria looks embittered, but she answers Leis regardless. Hearing her reply, he stares back at her with a distant look in his eyes and says, "Saving as many people as possible...really. I have already heard that your sense of virtue is so strong that you threw yourself into battle without concern for your own life. Apparently, the rumor is true. Can I respectfully ask the reason for your devotion to righteousness?"

After a lengthy pause, Aria begins speaking slowly.

"...A number of years ago, when I was still a child, my hometown was attacked by a demon army. Amid the confusion, I wandered off with my mother, but a demon captured us. But...just when I thought we were going to die, she appeared before us: the beautiful, virtuous elf the Holy Blade!"

"The Holy Blade...the same person who single-handedly defeated the demon army that fell upon the elf homeland Lumilus and, according to one theory, smashed a pillar of the great demon lord... That Holy Blade? I see—you were enamored with her after she saved your life and decided to travel down the path of righteousness... Is that correct?"

"Yes. I am still far from the strength that the Holy Blade possesses, but someday, I promise to save many people, just like she did...!"

"Saving many people...is an incredible goal in life..."

Realizing that Leis had fallen silent and was staring at her, Aria stammers, "A-anyway, you haven't ogled Stella or me even once. That makes us so happy. Almost every man we encounter looks at us like pieces of meat..."

"Ha-ha! Well, yes, that's true. If I looked at you in that way, my fiancée would not be very pleased with me."

"Oh, you have a fiancée? She must be just as lovely as you."

"Yes, of course. She has chestnut brown hair and a gentle smile, a heart so big that she's kind to everyone, and she loves flowers. She is always looking after me... It's certainly wasted on a man like myself..."

"...?"

Aria now has a sense of Leis's amiable nature, and the reason that she doesn't feel him leering at her is because of his fiancée. In the same moment, she experiences a strange sensation at his reply, because when he spoke, he stared up at the stars as if remembering his fiancée like a whisper of the past.

"...To tell the truth, she got upset with me a number of times during our dates because I was clearly distracted by other women. She was incensed and wouldn't listen to a word I said for a while. However, when I traveled deep into the forest to find her favorite flowers and gave them to her, she forgave me somehow."

"Hee-hee! Well, it sounds like you deserved to be in the doghouse."

Realizing that Aria is staring at him, puzzled, Leis is taken aback and recounts a memory of his fiancée getting upset with him. Aria laughs wryly at his story. Tama chimes in by nodding repeatedly, almost as if interjecting in the conversation.

"At any rate, this elemental cat of yours is truly a sagacious being."

Seeing Tama nodding, Leis changes the subject to him.

Did I say something wrong?

Aria wonders as Leis changes the subject suddenly. She decides not to dig any deeper, answering, "Tama is especially intelligent. He seems to fully understand human conversation, and he has a number of innate skills."

"Wow, does that mean others in addition to the elemental attacks I witnessed this afternoon?"

"I have confirmed a number of them, but I don't think he has any close-quarter-combat skills. Then again...he has a habit of hiding his abilities from me, so I can't really be certain..."

So far, Tama has unleashed unbelievable skills at the very last minute, and Aria looks at him reproachfully. He merely shakes his head—"Meown?"—and feigns ignorance.

"Okay then, Leis. We've finished our dinner, so let's get ready for bed— Oh? What's that sound?"

Just as Aria suggests bedding down for the night to Leis, the focus of her protection, she hears a strange noise.

Leis and Stella look at Aria quizzically—they don't hear anything. However...

It sounds like something being dragged along the ground...and something heavy...

Tama can hear it, too.

The cat (behemoth) Tama and the elf Aria have far superior hearing compared to normal humans. They cannot ignore the far-off sound.

"It's coming closer quickly. Tama, Stella, prepare for battle!"

"Meown!" *You got it, master!*

"Hmph! I don't care what kind of monster it is; I'll rip it to shreds!"

Aria grabs her knives, and Stella hoists her Mega Shield and greatsword, both in full battle-ready position. Leis moves to the rear of the party so he can escape at a moment's notice.

"Meown—!" *Divine Lion Protection!*

This time around, Tama activates Divine Lion Protection on everyone before the enemy can get close.

Leis exclaims in wonder. "Wow! This is incredible—I've been given night vision!"

Tama has activated Divine Lion Protection to increase everyone's physical capacity, but night vision is the primary reason he used it.

Aria speaks out, saying, "That's a...small treant, right? I've seen them in my studies before."

The tree monster slowly creeping toward them is called a small treant, approximately ten feet long and relying on skills and the hefting of its body on top of enemies to attack.

Puzzled, Leis remarks, "This is strange. There shouldn't be any small treants inhabiting this region..."

Normally, small treants appear only in forests or forest labyrinths, and to the party's knowledge, there is no such place nearby.

"Don't think too hard about this one, Tama! It's time for you to burn this thing to a crisp with your Flame Howl!"

"Meown—!" *Leave it to me, master! Flame Howl!*

Tama answers Aria with an adorable meow and activates Flame Howl, one of his Elemental Howls.

"*Grrr-awwwwrrr—!!*"

The small treant screams in utter agony along the night road.

Tama's Flame Howl has the fearsome capacity to completely evaporate a troll's life force. The small treant's wooden body was instantly engulfed in flame and burned to ashes and dust.

Suddenly, Leis yells, "Oh my god...! This is bad, Aria. There are a number of them flanking from the rear!"

Just as he said, a herd of small treants is encroaching on the party. One, two, three... There must be at least ten of them.

"Let's prepare the carriage! Traveling by night is dangerous, but there could be even more coming!"

"Understood!"

At Aria's command, Leis packs into the carriage as she jumps into the driver's seat. Tama hops onto Aria's shoulder and readies himself to attack monsters at any time.

Stella gets onto the cargo platform with her sword brandished, prepared to leap out as necessary.

"Meown—!" *Divine Lion Protection!*

Tama activates the powerful buff skill again—this time on the six carrier lizards supporting their carriage. He's given them night vision to navigate the dark path.

"Hahhh—!!"

Aria cracks the lead, and the carrier lizards cry out and stampede forth as the small treants all scream, *"Grrr-awwwwrrr—!!"* They're upset their prey is escaping.

"Is this...?"

"It's...a forest, I think? It's growing very close to the road."

Leis responds to Aria's query from inside the carriage. A while after setting forth with the carrier lizards, they came across a number of small treants, but Tama either annihilated them with Elemental Howls or Stella split them in half with her greatsword.

Now, a forest looms in front of the party, and it isn't included anywhere on their map.

Shrill cries erupt from the tree line.

"Keekeeee—!"

Immediately after, a seven-foot-tall monkey monster flies out of the darkness.

"It's a giant ape...!"

Aria's eyes go wide as saucers at the monkey monster—a giant ape—coming toward them. They are formidable creatures, well-known for the pleasure they take in causing pain to humans.

However, that's not the reason Aria is in shock. Giant apes should also appear only in forest labyrinths or areas near one. However, this one flew directly out of the forest... In other words—

"Is this forest a labyrinth in itself—?"

From within the carriage, Leis is the one to verbalize Aria's and Tama's suspicions.

"Let's forget about that for now. Stella, can you handle this?"

"Hmph, being of use to you offends me, but I do feel like causing a ruckus. I will accept and show you how it's done!"

As she speaks, Stella leaps from the cargo platform. At the same moment, her body morphs into dragonewt form, increasing her menace.

"Meown!" *Divine Lion Protection!*

Tama jumps down behind Stella. Giant apes are C-ranked monsters. They may not be a challenge for Stella, but Tama has cast a buff to bring up their base-level skills. He's prepared to serve as backup and hasn't forgotten to be ready to cast an Elemental Howl whenever necessary.

"Keekeeeeeee!"

The giant ape brings a fist down in a rush, but Stella welcomes and deflects it with her Mega Shield.

Bonnng—!

The creature's fist and her Mega Shield collide in a thundering echo.

"Rrrngah—!"

Stella's expression is indescribable as she whips her shield from side to side. The giant ape's eyes widen in shock as it realizes that tiny little Stella has blocked its fist smash like a falling feather.

Stella's prowess with her shield has increased even further. Until now, she's been able to use her shield only as a blunt instrument, but at this point, she has developed more advanced attack techniques.

That makes all the difference.

In a single flash, her greatshield rips across in a perfect horizontal line, splitting the giant ape's belly in half.

"Leis, if this forest is indeed a brand-new labyrinth that's just been conceived…"

"It would be a magnificent treasure trove for any adventurers who found it, I'm sure."

It is possible for labyrinths to suddenly appear in places where there was nothing before. Labyrinths that have just been conceived into existence are wholly untouched, filled with valuable materials and treasure boxes the likes of which one hears of only in fairy tales.

For any adventurer who fancies getting rich quickly, such labyrinths are like a dream.

However, first we must deliver the earth dragon skeleton and Leis safely to Gladstone.

Aria is highly attracted to the prospect of a newly conceived labyrinth, but as an adventurer, she must properly carry out the quest with which she's been entrusted.

Though painfully reluctant, Aria puts Stella and Tama back in the carriage, and the party leaves the newfound forest in their wake.

Just before dusk—

"Phew, we managed to arrive safely somehow. I must express my thanks to you, Aria, Stella, and Tama."

Leis offers his thanks to his escorts at the entrance to Gladstone, their final destination. They'd encountered a number of monsters, were ambushed in the middle of the night, and what they thought to be a labyrinth had appeared suddenly along their path—without Aria's quick decision-making, Stella's battle prowess, and the night vision bestowed upon them by Tama's Divine Lion Protection, he likely wouldn't have made it safely.

"Not at all. This is our profession. For now, let's proceed and deliver the earth dragon skeleton to your company storehouse. Afterward, in the morning, we'll have to inform the guild of our quest completion and about the labyrinth that cropped up so close to the road."

"It's just that...but, Aria, how would you feel about heading back to the labyrinth right away?"

"...Are you sure?"

Aria's response is immediate.

"Of course. Once we deliver the skeleton, my employees will begin unloading it. You've been a great service to me, and I would love for you to make some money from that untouched labyrinth."

Any adventurer would die to enter a virgin labyrinth, and Leis understands this as he makes his proposal.

"In that case...we'd love to take you up on that."

"Please, please. If it suits you, you may bring whatever materials you collect back to my company storehouse. I'd love to study them with you!"

"That would be a great help... Stella, Tama, do you have another one in you?"

"Meown—!" *You got it, master!*

"No problem at all! If anything, after our battles thus far, I'm on fire and want to crush some skulls!"

Tama and Stella are both ready to rock. Stella doesn't quite understand the allure of an unexplored labyrinth, but that's no bother.

"Aria, if you'd like, I will loan you a carrier lizard. Because it's dangerous out there, please command it to return here before you arrive. That does mean you'll have to walk home..."

"Thank you! That will be more than satisfactory."

At Aria's reply, Leis smiles cheerfully and sends the party on their way. "Okay then, I will wish for your triumphant return."

Seeing his smile, Aria again senses a dark shadow or hint of remorse...something just not quite right. Yet, at this juncture, she can't let it bother her too much, because in addition to the chance to delve into what they believe to be an untouched labyrinth, she will have the opportunity to sell the materials gathered to a merchant without the guild as an intermediary.

Going through the guild means paying a commission. With a direct merchant connection, she'll be able to profit without any extra fees.

Aria is not particularly greedy. In the future, she wants to travel the world as a warrior of justice. To this end, she believes she'll need to establish several bases for herself across the land.

Furthermore, she requires a decent amount of savings to apply to Stella's future.

From these two perspectives, venturing into the labyrinth they've discovered is now her number one priority. Even on the off chance that someone else gets there before them, if the labyrinth has indeed just been conceived recently, they will be able to make a generous profit.

"Tama, Stella—let's drink a stamina potion while we're at it."

While swaying back and forth on the carrier lizard's back, Aria reaches into her leather satchel and brings out two magic stamina potions that heal exhaustion. She gives one to Tama perched between her breasts and the other to Stella sitting behind her.

"Gehhh—this is so bitter! But I do feel less tired...?"

Stella furrows her brow at the bitter potion and is perplexed to find that it already seems to be working. It's no surprise, given she was a monster in her past life, so healing exhaustion with an item is definitely a first for her.

All right—I was getting sleepy, but with this, I should be fine.

The behemoth cub Tama was due for an afternoon nap, but thanks to the stamina potion, he's fully alert.

As Tama suckles the bottle and drinks it down, Aria thinks:

Ohhh... It's like he's sucking a nipple... It's turning me on! ♡

Her mind begins heading in a certain direction…but let's forget that for now.

❖

Hmm. It seems nobody has actually set foot in here. Surely master will be pleased.

Tama realizes it's very likely that nobody has entered before them. After doing some reconnaissance, the party finds nothing but grass and trees, along with one spot that could possibly serve as an entrance or exit.

They work feverishly to cut away the brush and attempt to enter, but an invisible wall prevents them from going any farther. The party surmises that a barrier of sorts separates the interior of the labyrinth from the outside world.

This labyrinth isn't an underground cave like the one in Labyrinthos, so they were excited to delve inside, but they aren't having any luck currently.

Aria isn't aware of it, but only in very rare cases do labyrinths have more than a single way to enter and escape.

The party is unable to confirm any footprints around the spot they've found, the presumed sole entrance. In other words, they're treating it as proof that nobody has been in the area.

And this sensation…it's the bloodlust monsters emanate. This has to be a labyrinth.

Tama's feral instincts convince him of this fact.

"Hmph, I can smell a bunch of pitiful small fry."

"I agree; I can feel the presence of monsters. I realize you're tough, Stella, but don't let your guard down, got it?"

Stella was a dragon in a past life, and Aria was born and raised in the outdoors. They've both recognized the aura of monsters hanging in the air inside the forest.

Stella's mouth twists into a delighted grin while Aria rubs her arm in anxiety about the upcoming battle.

"Meown—"

"Ohhh, Tama...you're encouraging me, aren't you?"

Tama nuzzles his head against Aria's cheek from his perch in between her breasts, trying to lift her spirits. Aria's shoulders drop and relax in response to his tender concern.

"Grrrr... Why only you, always, Aria?! No fair!"

"Stella, this time around, we don't have Vulcan with us, so we need to cooperate even more than before."

"Hmph, if you want us to fight together so badly, then you'll have to do it on my terms."

Stella doesn't give a rat's ass about Aria's words of admonishment. Once she realized that Aria is weaker than she is, her attitude toward the elf turned pompous and hasn't changed in the few days since.

This is not ideal... Even though we have the rare chance to delve into an untouched labyrinth, we might end up having to fall back immediately... I wish there was a way to resolve this— Wait a minute!

As Aria racks her brain for a way to get Stella to cooperate, one particular idea flashes into her mind...

"Tama? You definitely prefer girls who cooperate with others to fight, right? Not girls who just go wild all on their own?"

Aria turns to Tama and speaks to him with a loving smile. Seeing this unfold, Stella's eyes grow wide in surprise.

S-so that's what you're after, master... You're going to use me as bait to get Stella to listen to what you're saying, right? It's a bit awkward taking advantage of Stella's feelings like that...but what other choice do we have?

Tama has read Aria's intentions and come to a conclusion—

"Meown—!" *Of course, master!* Tama mews adorably and nods to show his agreement.

"Grrrrrrrrrr—! I've changed my mind! I will fight alongside you, Aria! I am a girl who can cooperate with others in battle!"

The result is immediate.

Stella had been tromping on ahead by herself, but she now rushes back to Aria and hoists her shield, as if covering Aria.

"Hee-hee... Tama, it looks like Stella wants to work together after all! Isn't that great news?"

"M-meown—!" *Master, I didn't know you could be so ruthless...,* Tama thinks.

"Okay, for now let's keep pushing forward... But first, can you put a buff on us, Tama? It's to enhance all our faculties, but also, this is a forest labyrinth. There will likely be mid-level monsters that can cause status ailments dwelling within."

Wow...master, you knew that could happen? It's apparent that you've been brushing up on your monster and labyrinth knowledge with Vulcan during your daytime study sessions.

Tama is impressed.

Until now, Aria has been invested only in refining her own skills. After forming a party with Vulcan, though, she's been learning so many things that have proven indispensable when fighting monsters or venturing into a labyrinth.

Partially thanks to this, the Aria who previously couldn't tell the difference between a regular goblin and its mutated form, a goblin mage—and was ambushed as a result—can now calmly approach a brand-new challenge standing before her.

And that isn't all—Aria has also absorbed some of Vulcan's battle strategy know-how. This is why the party was able to complete their mission, despite a number of incidents along the way. She's also succeeded in reining in Stella.

Aria is starting to develop as a person, not just as a warrior. Tama almost feels like he's watching his daughter growing up—it's a warm, fuzzy, and proud feeling.

"Meown—!" *Okay then, Divine Lion Protection!*

Tama cries out, and a bright golden aura envelops Tama, Aria, and Stella. All three of the party members receive dramatic buffs, allowing them to protect themselves from the monsters they were worried about—those that cause status ailments.

Not to mention, this labyrinth is filled with thick brush, and hardly any light can enter from outside. Their field of vision would normally be extremely limited, but the night-vision effect provided by Divine Lion Protection allows them to proceed with ease.

"Ki-ki—!"

"Ki-kiiii—!!"

A few minutes' walk into the labyrinth, two giant apes appear in front of Aria and company.

"Well hello there, ape brutes! I'll slice you to ribbons with my sword—or whatever, just bring it on!"

Stella instantly races forward to attack but then suddenly stops in place. She hoists her Mega Shield, ready to strike at any time.

Tama thinks, *Well isn't that something...*, and is impressed. He was convinced that Stella was all talk and that, when she had the chance, she would instantly rush out to attack with abandon.

However, it turns out Stella's desire to be loved by Tama is not superficial or halfhearted. As a dragon—an all-powerful being—even if she must cast her pride aside, she wants to fight alongside Aria and win Tama's affection.

"Tama, first and foremost, let's see what kinds of combo attacks Stella and I can do! Please support us when you see an opening!"

"Meown—!" *Roger that, master!*

Tama mews in affirmation and hops out from between Aria's breasts down onto the floor. In the same moment, the giant apes rush forward —one heading toward Stella and the other toward Aria.

"In that case...ummm, let's try this!"

Stella transforms into her dragonewt form in the face of the giant ape bounding at her and unleashes a shield-bash attack.

The beast is forcefully blasted backward. Seeing this, its companion recoils in surprise, stopping in its tracks for just a moment.

"Nice one, Stella!"

In the brief opening this causes, Aria activates her Acceleration skill and gives her movement a speed boost.

And then—*whoosh*! Aria races forward and steps inside the giant ape's stance, stabbing forward with her knife and aiming for the heart.

"*Gi-iiiiii—!!*"

The giant ape screams in the throes of death. It flexes both arms and uses all its strength in an attempt to strangle Aria, yet—

"Meown—!" *No chance!*

Tama is watching vigilantly and activates Summon Tentacle to wrap up the giant ape's arms. It resists in vain and collapses to the ground.

"T-Tama…! Send me some tentacles, too!"

—*You got it, Stella!*

Stella calls out to Tama, and he answers her through telepathy.

The first giant ape is just standing up as Tama sends tentacles to trap it.

"You're finished—!!"

Stella growls, rushes forward, and raises her greatsword toward the immobilized giant—the battle has been won. She feels extremely awkward, but in terms of properly cooperating, she has likely cleared with a passing grade.

"Good job, Stella! You did a great job for disliking working together so much!"

"H-hmph! It's not for your sake, Aria. I only did it to show Tama that I'm a girl who can cooperate for the benefit of her party members!"

"Hee-hee! You can be so cute, Stella."

Aria's approval of Stella's diligent partnership must have embarrassed the former earth dragon, as her cheeks flush red. She did it for Tama, but being praised by Aria makes her a bit happy, too.

—*Stella, great job. Keep it up.*

—*T-Tama, you're praising me, too? Okay, you got it!*

Tama's telepathic message of support instantly lights up Stella's eyes. Her face blossoms into a smile that makes her look so much like a cute young girl, one would easily forget that she was an oversized lizard in her past life.

Hmm... Stella and Tama are staring at each other silently again. Just what is going on between them?

Watching from the side, Aria notices Tama and Stella seemingly staring into each other's eyes, and feeling a tinge of jealousy, the elf puffs out her cheeks.

But let's forget that for now. Aria shakes it off and switches gears, looking down at the corpses of the giant apes at her feet.

"Normally, I'd like to skin their hides and bring them back with us, but there's a limit to what will fit in my backpack, and since it will be cumbersome as we delve deeper, I guess we'll have to give up on that..."

Aria casts her gaze away from the giant ape corpses and sighs heavily. A giant ape hide will fetch a considerable price when sold. She wants to take them with her but also doesn't want to be encumbered as they progress through the labyrinth. Plus, they might find some treasure boxes.

Aria and Stella are both wearing backpacks, but they want to refrain from collecting too much baggage right away.

Hmm... Giant ape hides... Leaving them behind is definitely a waste. I know—I'll put a new skill on display. If we're asking Leis to purchase the items, I'm sure he'll keep the skill a secret for me, too.

Tama has made up his mind and approaches Aria's feet, mewing at her.

"What's up, Tama?"

"Meown—!" *She's looking at me. Activate skill: Storage!*

"Wha—?! The giant ape corpses completely disappeared!"

"Just what does this mean?!"

As Tama activates his skill Storage, the giant ape corpses disappear into thin air. Aria's and Stella's eyes are wide as saucers in surprise. However, Aria quickly realizes something is up and looks back at Tama, as if saying, *Tama...it was you, wasn't it?*

"Meown—!" *You know it, master!*

Tama mews while nodding and activates Storage again. This time, the giant ape corpses he just stowed away reappear in front of them.

"T-Tama, were you hiding this skill from me, too...? Once again, you are such an incredible kitty."

"That was amazing! I knew you were the mate for me!"

The skill Storage is extremely rare, often said to be one in a million. The amount of items that can be tucked away varies by user, and Aria has heard that, in most cases, the skill is usually limited to small items. For Tama to be able to stow away two entire massive giant ape corpses...

Aria stares at him, slack-jawed, while Stella loudly exclaims just how amazing he is.

"If Tama has this skill, we won't need to leave anything behind! Tama, is there still room for more items using your skill?"

"Meown—!" *Don't worry—there's plenty of room, master!*

"Okay—let's keep on going!"

"Aria, why do you look so happy?"

"Stella, selling monster corpses earns us money. With more money, we can eat a whole bunch of delicious food!"

"Say what?! Aria, you must tell me these things sooner! Yes! We will kill many monsters and eat lots and lots of delicious food!"

Aria's simple explanation has Stella's eyes burning brighter than ever before. Her mind is filled with images of all the food she's eaten in the past few days.

Aria leads her along as they march farther into deeper recesses of the labyrinth. It's certainly a forest—thick brush threatens to conceal their path forward, and the configuration would leave anyone who lets their guard down for just a moment lost.

Without Aria's superior sense of direction honed from her upbringing in the wild, the party would have likely already lost track of the labyrinth's exit.

Additionally, this place has a very particular aura. Traversing the entire perimeter of the labyrinth from the outside didn't take long at all, but no matter how deep they go inside, they can't catch a single glimpse of the outside world.

"Tama! Please use Aether Howl!"

"Meown—!" *Leave it to me, master! Aether Howl!*

At Aria's request, Tama unleashes his Elemental Howl, Aether Howl. He's aiming for two massive hornet enemies diving down on Aria and Stella with their stingers. They're as big as a human head and called poison bees—C-ranked monsters in terms of danger.

Just as their name states, the stingers on their rear ends contain a poison that not only quickly drains their victims' life forces but also causes confusion. They're a truly bothersome monster.

Thanks to the effects of Divine Lion Protection cast on the girls by Tama, the poison won't have any affect, but being stung in a vital spot is very dangerous regardless.

Landing a hit on the poison bees buzzing around them with her throwing knives is a nearly impossible task for Aria. This is why she's asked Tama to attack them with Aether Howl, a wide-range skill.

Wrhoosh—!

Tama mews adorably and sends a powerful blast of air rushing above Aria's and Stella's heads. The poison bees are blasted off-balance a split second before landing their attacks and are blasted off course, crashing on the ground.

"That's it—Acceleration!"

"No way they'll take us down!"

Aria immediately boosts her speed with Acceleration and chases the poison bees. Thanks to the added effects of Tama's Divine Lion Protection, Aria is faster than a speeding bullet.

Stella also activates her dragonewt form and gains incredible speed, although she's not quite as fast as Aria in front of her.

Bzz-bzzzz... The poison bees' wings flap wildly in an attempt to right themselves and fly. However, due to the damage taken when they were blasted against the ground, neither can get airborne.

Shrrrring—!

A fierce shrill pierces the air—Aria has sliced the first bee directly in half horizontally. The sharpness of Aria's *tamahagane*-and-orichalcum-alloy blade combined with her speed makes it a piece of cake.

"Not letting you get away!"

Just as the second poison bee seems like it will succeed in taking flight, Stella uses the hilt of her greatsword to smash it flat.

"Oh, what a waste!" Aria moans. Poison bee wings and stingers can be sold for a decent price—her reaction is understandable given that the monster is now flat as a pancake.

Mm? What's this presence...?

As Aria pouts, Tama senses another unknown being.

"There's something hiding in this brush!"

"It seems like you're right. Stella, I'll attack with a throwing knife. When the enemy jumps out in surprise, I want you and Tama to attack!"

Stella and Aria can feel the presence drifting out from the brush, too. Aria gives Stella and Tama their orders and removes a knife from her garter belt to throw it in the enemy's direction when...

"Wahhh! Halt, human! I'm not your enemy!"

"That's right! Please don't attack us!"

Two adorable, tiny voices can be heard from within the brush.

"Who are you? Show yourselves!"

"O-okay, we'll come out."

"Wahhh, wait, don't leave me behind—!"

In response to Aria's demand, two different voices can be heard as the creatures emerge from their hiding spot.

"W-wait...a pixie? For real?"

"Meown—!" *And a dryad, too?!*

Aria and Tama cannot hide their abject surprise at the two newcomers. One of them, a tiny peach-colored creature with wings on her back, is small enough to fit in the palm of a human hand.

The other is the size of a little girl with dark-green hair and eyes and light-green skin.

"Yep! I'm a pixie! Lily's my name!"

"And I'm a dryad named Feri. Pleased to make your acquaintance."

The winged girl sniffs proudly, and the green-skinned girl quietly introduces herself.

"A pixie and a dryad? What are they? Delicious?"

"Stella, they aren't food. They're both types of fairies who live in forests and forest labyrinths. I've only ever seen them in my study materials..."

Stella looks perplexed as she asks about the two creatures, prompting Aria's explanation. The elf looks happy, in a sense. Just as she said, Lily and Feri are a pixie and a dryad, both members of the fairy family. They are extremely rare, and even if you come across one, they usually run away immediately.

However, if they do show themselves, whoever beholds them is said to receive a great fortune.

"Ah-ha-ha! And look at you—such an interesting little fella, aren'tcha?"

"Yeah, you're so small and fluffy and cute!"

While Aria gives her fairy lesson, Lily and Feri both come closer to Tama, wide-eyed with curiosity.

Feri reaches out and scoops up his tiny body. Lily yells out, "Wheeee—!" and flies onto his back, rolling around in his fuzzy fur.

"M-meown—?"

Tama isn't sure how to respond to the two tiny creatures suddenly playing with him and mews awkwardly.

"Ummm… You said your names are Lily and Feri, right? This is Tama. My name is Aria, and this girl here is Stella. It seems that you were observing us from within the brush. Is there something you want with us?"

"Ah-ha-ha, his name is Tama! His name is just as cute as he is!"

"So your names are Aria and Stella. We were watching you because Tama is so cute, we wanted to be friends with him…"

"No, it's because whatever you have in your bag smells so good, Aria! Won't you give us a little bit?"

While they play with Tama and pet his fluffy fur, Lily and Feri answer Aria's question in turn.

"Something in my bag…? Could it possibly be this?"

Aria takes a small container out of her bag and opens the lid. The sweet aroma that wafts from it elicits goofy grins on Lily's and Feri's faces.

"Ahhh! I want some!"

"My goodness, what a lovely smell!"

The food Lily and Feri are going crazy over is fruit preserved in honey. It seems they both were entranced by its fragrance and have been following Aria and company.

"Hee-hee, you're both so cute. Please have some."

""Yayyy—!!""

Lily and Feri lunge at the container containing the honey-preserved fruit as soon as Aria offers it to them. Feri digs in with her hands but brings the fruit to her mouth with a delicate elegance. Lily picks up a piece with the strength of her tiny body and nibbles on it excitedly.

"Wooow—Feri, human food is so good, isn't it?!"

"Yeah, you're right—and it's been so long since we had food a human prepared!"

Lily and Feri banter while devouring the honey-preserved fruit almost immediately.

Aria realizes something from their conversation and asks the girls a question.

"Does that mean you've met other humans before? This labyrinth is newly formed, so there shouldn't be any other humans who've set foot in here…"

"'*Newly formed*'? You mean…?"

"Maybe this place reincarnated again?"

Lily and Feri turn to look at each other while they speak.

"The labyrinth reincarnated… Does that mean this is a 'reborn labyrinth'?"

There are a number of different types of labyrinths. There are those like the one in Labyrinthos that stay in the same place and continuously generate monsters. Some can also be relocated in space and time, and others, for unknown reasons, can be reborn once their initial purpose as a labyrinth has been fulfilled, at which point all their internal characteristics reset. That's the *"reborn labyrinth"* that Aria mentioned.

"That's exactly right! Hey, human—I mean, Aria, if you want, we can guide you through this labyrinth. How about it?"

"Ohhh! Really? Are you sure, Lily?"

"Of course—! You gave us delicious food. We want to become friends with Tama, and you guys definitely don't look like bad people!"

Feri's kind reply prompts Aria to quickly accept Lily's sudden proposal. It seems both fairies are very interested in Tama.

While they chat, the two start petting Tama's fluffy fur again.

"Grrrrr—! And I'm still not allowed to hold Tama! Get away from him, you little scamps!"

"Wahhh—! I thought she was just mad, but she literally transformed!"

"She looks just like a dragon!"

Seeing Lily and Feri playing with Tama as much as they want, Stella's jealousy boils over. She's transformed into her dragonewt form and is frantically trying to chase them away.

—*Stella, that's enough!*

—*Erk. Tama…*

Just as Lily and Feri start shuddering in fear, Tama attempts to defuse the situation through telepathy. A direct command from Tama will quell even the fiery Stella.

She reluctantly disengages her dragonewt form.

"Well, there's no other way around it. I concede—once we finish clearing this labyrinth and arrive back in Gladstone, I'll let you hold Tama just once, okay, Stella?"

Wh-what are you saying, master?! Don't be hasty…!

Tama is taken aback at Aria's promise, and his eyes go wide as saucers.

"What?! Are you serious, Aria?!"

"It will be a reward for cooperating and fighting with us. But only once, you got it?"

"This is excellent news! Okay, little pixie and dryad. Hurry up and show us the way so we can get out of here quickly!"

Aria and Stella have hatched their accord without any regard for Tama's feelings. He sighs, *Oh, master…*, as he watches how accustomed Aria has become to controlling Stella using him as bait.

However, hearing that this is a one-time offer, Tama also realizes that Aria still considers Stella, another woman, a threat…

"In that case, we'll guide you! Tama, when we finish the labyrinth, you have to become our friend, okay?"

"Petting Tama's fluffy fur feels so good!"

Lily and Feri are obliged to help Aria and company, if only for the sake of befriending Tama.

A fairy's senses are difficult to comprehend. However, for the party, this is an unexpected windfall—they're delving into an untouched labyrinth with two fairy girls as navigators, after all.

"Okay, so what kind of items are you after?"

"Yeah, are you in the market for monster hides or medicinal herbs?"

"Both are tempting, but what I really want is a treasure box. Have you seen any highly decorated chests before?"

When Lily and Feri ask what kind of items Aria is after, she expresses her desire for a treasure box.

In an untouched labyrinth, the chances of finding one shouldn't be too low—at least, that's Aria's impression.

"If that's what you're after, we definitely saw one, right, Feri?"

"Yep, you're right, Lily. Okay then, we'll guide you to it!"

The little fairies' reaction confirm the elf's hunch.

Aria is uncontrollably happy and scoops up Tama, exclaiming, "Yes! We did it!" as she squeezes him tightly against her breasts.

"Meown—!" *Aqua Howl!*

Some time passes after the party delves deeper into the labyrinth following Lily and Feri's navigation—and four small treants appear. They must have picked up on Aria and company's scent.

Small treants look like plant monsters, but they are carnivorous and violent. They've targeted the adventurers to eat their flesh.

Tama activates one of his Elemental Howls, Aqua Howl, against a small treant. He's aiming for the thick, armlike branches on both sides of the monsters. His high-pressure blast of water rushes against the appendages and rips them to shreds.

"Wooow, that's amazing, Tama!"

"He's so strong for being such a tiny little cutie!"

Lily and Feri rave excitedly—they can't believe that Tama has such incredible battle prowess, even though he's so fluffy and cute.

In reality, Tama could use Flame Howl instead of Aqua Howl

to torch the small treants and clean them up all at once, but he chooses not to given that this is a forest labyrinth. If he uses fire-based skills here, the entire area will go up in a sea of flames.

"*Gi-gyaaaa—!*"

The small treant erupts in a scream of pain at having its branches blasted off—or was it anger? Probably both. The monster lashes out in a desperate final attack. Without its branches, that's its only option.

"I'll handle this!"

Stella steps up to the vanguard and faces the small treant. It's not exactly the ideal formation, but she raises her shield to protect Aria and Tama, intercepting the monster. Stella's Mega Shield and the small treant's trunk collide.

"*Giii—?!*"

The monster screams in shock as the entire weight of its sizable body is blocked easily by Stella and her tiny frame.

Stella ignores its reaction and puts all the strength she can muster into her Mega Shield, sending the creature flying backward. It loses its balance and falls to the ground, dragging the other treant behind it down with it.

"Meown—!" *Summon Tentacle!*

Tama activates his absorbed skill Summon Tentacle, and a number of tentacles sprout from the ground at lightning speed, successfully ensnaring the last two small treants rushing in from the rear.

"Time to die!!"

Stella brings her greatsword down with abandon on the pair of trapped small treants collapsed in front of her. With the other two trapped by Tama, she can obliterate the trunks of these ones without a care in the world. Stella tears into both at once, ripping through their midsections.

"*Gi-gyaaaa—!*"

Their death throes reverberate throughout the labyrinth.

In that moment, a shadowy figure rushes with blinding speed toward the two small treants entrapped by tentacles. Of course, it's Aria, who's activated Acceleration. She's holding her knives, specially made by Vulcan, in both hands. She approaches the immobilized small treants and thrusts her blades into a spot on the upper-left portion of their trunks.

Small treants have a core that is necessary for all their life functions, located in the same place as a human heart. Aria knows this—she's learned from Vulcan and studied the best way to deal with all sorts of monsters.

Without emitting a sound, the two small treants begin spasming wildly before suddenly falling on the ground with a thunderous crash.

"Phew! That wasn't exactly perfect, but with Stella as our tank, me as the ambush, and Tama as our support, our teamwork has reached new heights..."

After hearing that she'll have the chance to hold Tama, Stella is more motivated than ever and has performed her role as tank with ease. She's still treating enemies lurking in the rear as perfunctory and largely devoted to focusing her attacks on power, but Aria doesn't have any complaints about her general progress.

Her cooperation is more than enough for a labyrinth of this level, and with Tama's precise support, the party should be just fine. At this rate, Aria expects an even deeper level of collaboration moving forward.

When Vulcan, who's currently holding down the fort in Labyrinthos, joins them in the vanguard, they'll be able to take on their most optimal form yet.

"Whoaaa, that was a surprise! It's not just Tama—Aria and Stella, you're so strong, too!"

"Yeah, Aria's as fast as the wind, and Stella has the power of a dragon!"

As Aria sheathes her knives, Lily and Feri express their admiration.

"Before this labyrinth reincarnated, what sort of fighting styles did you see in other adventurers?"

Aria gets curious about Lily and Feri's conversation and asks the two fairies, who respond:

"Good question! All the people we watched from the shadows definitely worked together in battle!"

"Yes, and I don't think we've ever seen anyone like you guys, each with your own individual superior battle skills."

The girls haven't seen many parties that suddenly activated unique individual skills.

"But anyway! The treasure box you wanted, Aria—is that it?"

As she speaks, Lily points forward to a tiny ornate treasure box that would fit in Aria's hands, left behind carelessly.

"This is a treasure box…?"

Aria races forward toward it and slowly, cautiously reaches out her hand. Seeing this, Tama rushes to jump onto her shoulder, reminded of his experience discovering a Warp Crystal in the labyrinth in Labyrinthos and being teleported to a lower level. If that happened here, Aria would likely not return alive.

Aria takes the treasure box into both hands. It's made of gold and adorned with precious stones all over. The chest alone could garner an incredible profit.

"Ah-ha-ha-ha! Whenever humans find those chests, they all react the same way!"

"Yeah, Aria, you look so happy."

Seeing Aria shaking with excitement, Lily and Feri are thoroughly entertained. They've seen the same scene play out a number of times before this labyrinth reincarnated.

"Okay, let's open it! I wonder what's inside…"

Aria nervously opens the lid.

Seeing its contents, Stella says, "Whoa, it's so tiny, but the stuff inside is so shiny and pretty!"

The treasure box holds a small, clear glass bottle that contains a translucent blue liquid…and the liquid itself glitters like the Milky Way.

That color and that sparkle... Could it be?!

"Teardrops of Truth...?"

Just as Tama surmises what's in the bottle, Aria has the same realization. Teardrops of Truth—a most sacred magical potion that causes anyone who drinks even a single drop to reveal the underlying intentions and truths that lie in their heart, without any prevarication.

"I've heard that its method of refinement has never been known...and maybe this is why...?"

Aria closes her hand on the Teardrops of Truth, visibly shaking. Just as she claims, the method of refinement used to create this potion is unknown—which is why it is considered sacred.

The reason Aria speculated, *"...and maybe this is why?"* is that she surmises that perhaps Teardrops of Truth appear only in treasure boxes in labyrinths.

"Stella, you must never tell a single soul that we discovered this item, okay? If our adversaries find out about it, they will certainly come hunt us down."

The effects of Teardrops of Truth are powerful, and for this reason, the potion can be used for evil. Aria pushes the reality of how important it is for their adversaries to never know they have it, but Stella clearly grasps the seriousness of the situation, saying, "I am only interested in Tama and eating food, so I don't care at all about that silly liquid."

"Hey, Aria, you sure seem excited for some reason..."

"There are still more treasure boxes, you know?"

Aria's eyes practically beam at Lily's and Feri's claims.

Following the two fairies' lead, the party presses onward.

"Haaah—!"

Aria's powerful voice echoes across the labyrinth as she rushes forward with her innate speed. She's aiming to step inside the stance of a giant ape looming before her. With her rapid approach, the beast doesn't have the chance to move. It doesn't even matter. The ape already has a massive gash running across its stomach—an open wound caused by Stella's greatsword. In addition, Aria has stuck throwing knives in its shoulder and arm.

Squelllch—!

Aria takes a knife in her hand and plunges it into the weakened giant ape's heart.

"Wow, our collaborative powers are even more refined now!"

"Yeah! If we flip the switch, this is a cakewalk!"

Shortly after obtaining the Teardrops of Truth, Aria and company have come across a few monsters, but they've successfully taken them down by working together. It hasn't been very long, but their synergistic skills are increasing faster than the eye can perceive.

"Ummm, I think it was around here…"

"Look over there, Aria—!"

Feri's glance starts to dart around their area and Lily points in a specific direction, where another of the adorned boxes—a treasure box—lies waiting for them.

"Hee-hee, I wonder what will be in this one?"

Aria excitedly reaches her hand toward the chest. Of course, Tama is stuck right to her shoulder, a preventative measure in case the box contains a Warp Crystal.

This treasure box is really small, too.

"Is this…a key, I guess?"

Aria removes a small key-shaped item crafted from iron ore that fits in the palm of her hand. It must be a magic item. Sparkling blue ripples pulsate intermittently on its surface, spreading in all directions.

"Oh wow, that key was hidden in a treasure box?"

"What do you mean, *'that key'*? Does it fit into a door in the labyrinth, Lily?"

"Yes, it does. Because it's a magic item that unlocks the boss room!"

Aria is a bit shocked by Lily's explanation and she responds, "'*Boss room*'...?! That means that this isn't a multitiered labyrinth—and it explains why we haven't seen any stairwells."

A boss room is the space in a labyrinth where the strongest enemy lies in wait. In the labyrinth in Labyrinthos, this space is where Stella spent her time as an earth dragon.

Among the different types of labyrinths, there are multitiered versions where the monsters get stronger as you proceed down through the floors and single-tiered versions that don't have upper and lower levels. Because the latter doesn't have levels, most examples of single-tiered labyrinths have a separate space locked by a special door, known as a boss room.

The key that Aria has just found is the magic item required to enter that room.

"Lily, Feri—do you know what kind of monster the boss of this labyrinth is?"

"Ummm, it's like a huge tree monster... What did the last party of adventurers call it?"

"I think it was 'treant drake,' right?"

Lily and Feri confer to answer Aria's question.

A drake is a wingless dragon that walks on two legs. They're approximately fifteen to twenty feet long and exist in every possible elemental distinction. For this reason, their strength can vary in rank from C+ to B+, depending on their element.

"A drake, hmm... That shouldn't be too much of a problem for us..."

Aria ponders. If she can defeat a drake, she'll definitely make a lot of money from its materials. And that's not all—there is a high possibility that a treasure box containing high-ranked items can be found in the boss room.

Given these facts, Aria would love to take on the battle and collect the rewards. However...

"Let's call it a day for now. Everyone is getting pretty tired, and we have the key, so we don't need to worry about someone coming in and taking it."

Nice! I'm so impressed by my master stepping up to make tough calls.

Tama mews in admiration at Aria's decision-making and nods repeatedly.

Stella responds with a touch of dissatisfaction, saying, "Hmph. We're done already?" However, when Aria suggests they go back to the city and eat some delicious food, her eyes light up like stars, and she follows suit.

"Hey, Aria, bring us with you, too!"

"Yeah, now that we're friends with Tama, we don't want to leave his side!"

As they speak, Lily and Feri surround Tama and start rubbing his fluffy fur.

"Grrrr—! Get away from him! ...Although, since I'll get to hold him once when we're done, I'll tolerate this for now."

Stella gets jealous of Lily and Feri surrounding Tama, but remembering that Aria will allow her to hold him, she quickly concedes.

"Hmm, well, we do owe you, Lily and Feri, for showing us the way through the labyrinth..."

Aria looks at Tama, who's a bit troubled by Lily's and Feri's incessant touching, and mulls over her options.

The idea of Lily and Feri joining them is more than welcome. If they stick together, there's a good possibility the two will guide them through the labyrinth again in the future.

Above all else, Aria is quite fond of the pair of pure, adorable little fairies.

"Lily, Feri—you're welcome to tag along with us, but human cities can be very dangerous. Are you sure you still want to come?"

Just as Aria states, human civilization can be quite dangerous for fairies. Members of the fairy family are rare, and some megalomaniacs practice the buying and selling of them at high prices. This is not commendable behavior, but it isn't specifically outlawed, either.

Lily and Feri are particularly good-looking, even for fairies. If someone sees them, there's no guarantee they won't be preyed upon for their monetary value and sold for ransom.

"Not to worry!"

"Yeah, we have battle skills, too, and if you and Tama are with us, we'll be fine!"

Lily and Feri do their best to allay Aria's concern. It's certainly true that anyone living in a labyrinth needs a certain level of skills to survive. That means that Lily and Feri must have some degree of battle prowess.

"Understood. In that case, let's head to the city together! I'll get you both as much sweets as you want as a token of thanks for today."

"Yayyy!"

"That's the best news!"

The fairies are delighted by Aria's proposal. They prance around shouting with joy as they circle Tama.

They clearly love sweets just like little kids.

Hmm, looks like a group of adventurers. Heh-heh… They're glancing this way, surprised.

As Tama bounces up and down on Aria's jiggling breasts, he uses his superior vision to pick up on a group of individuals dressed like adventurers within the city limits. They've likely obtained information about the new labyrinth and are planning their own siege.

They thought they had the jump on fresh information, but seeing Aria and company coming from that direction, they're clearly shocked.

"Hey, you chumps, could you possibly have already dug into the labyrinth—? Wait, fairies?!"

As the man who looks like the leader approaches Aria to question her, he spies Lily and Feri following behind and goes into shock.

"Yes, we just investigated it now. We befriended these two along the way."

"Y-you became friends with fairies? And what's with the smug look? You must have really hit the jackpot..."

The male adventurer sees Aria looking jolly and gets the gist of the situation. He looks slightly dejected at not having been the first to explore the labyrinth.

"No matter! There's no way you scoured the entire thing with just the few of you. That means we still have a chance. Don't let it deter us, everyone! Gear up!"

""""Raaah!!"""""

The man is the leader after all. As he switches gears, he calls out to his followers to psyche themselves up and press onward. They're more than ready to rumble by now.

"Sorry to bother you."

"Not at all. The labyrinth is filled with small treants, giant apes, and poison bees. Make sure to be careful, okay?"

"Is that so? We owe you one for that bit of information. My name is Joey. If we meet in the city again, please let me buy you a drink."

"My name is Aria. This girl here is Stella, and this is Tama. These two are Lily and Feri."

After exchanging thanks and introductions, the two parties head their separate ways.

Having closely watched Joey from in between Aria's breasts, Tama thinks, *Hmm. This Joey character is certainly full of ambition, and he didn't seem to leer at my master. He's made a pretty good impression on me.*

"A kind welcome to you, Aria and Stella. I have heard all about you from our president. Please, this way."

Aria and her party have headed directly to Leis's company facility after returning to the city, where a woman dressed in office garb greets them warmly.

"It's so great to have you back, Aria, Stella, and Tama. How did everything go—? Huh?!"

Immediately after the group was welcomed inside by the office lady, Leis appears from the back with a cheerful smile on his face. However, just as he asks about the success of their journey into the labyrinth, he stops short and falls silent, eyes wide. He's looking directly at Lily and Feri—

"Leis...?"

"Ahhh...please forgive me. A pixie and a dryad—this is my first time seeing fairies with my own eyes..."

Aria reacts in puzzlement, but Leis quickly gets ahold of himself and smiles at Lily and Feri.

"We met these two in the labyrinth. It seems cute li'l Tama caught their attention, and they came with us all the way here."

"W-wow, it's rare for fairies to become so enamored... Well, at any rate, let's go ahead and appraise the items you collected from the labyrinth."

"Okay! Yes, please. We definitely acquired quite an assortment..."

At Leis's behest, Aria prods Tama to use his Storage skill, and he produces the different monster corpses they collected. Leis and his staff are surprised by Tama's Storage skill, but seeing the different monster corpses in such high quality, they quickly begin the work of appraising each item.

However, Aria and company don't notice. As Leis begins the appraisal process, his occasionally glances furtively back toward Lily and Feri. When he does, his eyes are tinged with an indescribable dread.

"Mwa-ha-ha, Tama is all mine…!"

In a room of an inn in Gladstone—

Stella is breathing quietly and murmuring in her sleep, looking content as can be. Tama is ensconced in her bountiful bosom, sleeping soundly…

After selling the monster raw materials they collected in the labyrinth at Leis's company storehouse, Aria and her party found a reasonably priced inn and decided to rest until the evening.

Stella immediately used the "Hold Tama Just Once Ticket" that Aria had bestowed upon her and was able to cradle and sleep with him, finally. Because Aria made the decision without consulting him, Tama attempted to resist, but…

The second he ran away from her, he saw how devastated Stella looked, and he gave in. As a virtuous, noble knight, Tama could not force a lady to tears, even if she had been a monster in a past life.

Stella had so eagerly yearned to hold Tama. She must have imitated Aria, because even though she has the heart of a monster, she gently held Tama with deep affection and stroked his head as she carried him into bed.

Seeing this, Aria was assured that Stella wouldn't actually make a move, and she let her guard down. Aria is also sleeping quietly and adorably in the bed next to them.

The pixie Lily is lying down to sleep on Aria's melons as they rise and fall, and the dryad Feri is right next to the elf, where she fits perfectly. The two fairies saw Aria and company resting comfortably and became quite sleepy themselves.

Lily and Feri are breathing quietly and peacefully like two contented children. They're both reposed in peace and security, thanks to Aria's soft, enveloping melons and her affectionate, saintly aura.

That evening—

"Oh! If it isn't Aria and her crew!"

"Hey, Joey, you're back from the labyrinth, I see."

After their naps, Aria and company set out to find a tavern to get a bite to eat. A voice quickly rang out to them from the corner—it's Joey, the adventurer they met on their way back from their adventure.

His face is red as he pours drinks for his comrades. Their expressions are all brimming with satisfaction. They likely didn't find as much as Aria and her party, but their harvest from the labyrinth must have been great.

"Given the promise I made this afternoon, why don't you join us for a drink?"

"Don't mind if we do, then."

Generally, Aria would never accept the invitation of a man, but given that Joey doesn't look at her lecherously and his party also contains female adventurers, she's decided it will be okay.

That said, even though master would usually partake in alcohol in this situation, tonight she's ordered a nonalcoholic drink. She's staying vigilant. That's a relief.

As Aria orders a juice, Tama nods repeatedly in satisfaction.

A while after Aria and company sit down, Lily and Feri cry out, eagerly seeing the food laid in front of them.

"Wow! What is this—?!"

"It's so sweet and fluffy and delicious!"

Lily and Feri squeal with similar glee once they've tasted their meal: a stack of pancakes covered in whipped cream and honey. They both wanted something sweet rather than vegetables or meat, so Aria ordered it for them.

Feri looks content as she holds her cheeks with her tiny hands, and Lily has taken flight from her overwhelming enthusiasm and buzzes around the room, flapping her wings.

"Meown—!" *This is so good!*

"Meat is the best!"

Next to Lily and Feri, Tama is stuffing his cheeks with roast meat that Aria cut into small bites for him, and Stella is tearing into a bone-in cut ravenously.

The waitress tells the party that the meat dish is the house specialty, marinated with a special sauce made from fruits and spices. It's second-to-none deliciousness, even compared with the food at the inn in Labyrinthos.

"So, Aria, you guys must have sold your materials directly to Master Leis at his company facility, right? That makes sense—the guild staff said they didn't remember buying anything from you or your party."

"Yes, we just happened to take on a quest to escort Leis, and thanks to that connection, we were able to sell directly. By the way, Leis looked a little bit off earlier, and I'm worried about him…"

Aria smacks her lips while enjoying the meal and raises her concern with Joey. She recalls Leis's flustered temperament at his facility and once again worries if something is the matter.

"*A little bit off,*' huh…? Maybe he was remembering the past again?"

"The past? Joey, what happened?"

"Hmm, well, if you're going to be staying in this city, for your own safety, you should probably know the facts… I'll need to keep my voice down about this, but the lord of this city—the Earl of Gladstone—is a real indomitable son of a bitch. If he sees a pretty young woman, he'll use any means necessary to abduct her and abuse her in whatever ways he desires."

Joey speaks to Aria in a hushed tone as his eyes dart around the room.

Aria responds, "The earl would do such a thing?" in shock and asks why such actions would be tolerated.

"It's not that anyone actually tolerates it. It's just that the earl has a litany of scurvy tricks up his sleeve. He never leaves behind decisive evidence, and if anyone tries to speak up, he uses his position to silence them real quick."

"How can such a person be the lord...and how does this relate to Leis?"

"I've only heard this secondhand, so I don't know all the details, but apparently, Master Leis's fiancée was abducted by the earl. And after a while, one day...her corpse turned up, mutilated beyond recognition...at Leis's home."

"......"

Aria falls silent when Joey finishes speaking.

Leis's smile is so cheerful—Aria cannot believe the horrors he's experienced.

Next to Aria, Tama stopped eating once he got absorbed in the story.

"Sorry to raise such a strange topic. Let's drink up! You best believe we're getting the tab tonight."

Joey apologizes for creating a tense and awkward atmosphere and orders a new round of drinks to help the group get back to feeling good again.

Aria laughs in response, but deep down, she just can't manage to enjoy this party.

"Heh-heh-heh-heh..."

Leis chuckles in his moonlit company facility. He's gripping a magic item in each of his hands. In the right, he holds an object resembling a silver bell, and in his left, a reddish-black arrow—

"I never thought that, after so many years, I would obtain these two items from the skeleton of an earth dragon, but what's more, a pixie and a dryad have appeared... What incredible timing..."

Leis speaks quietly as he looks toward the earth dragon corpse stashed away in the rear of his storehouse. In the next moment, his face twists into an unbelievably contorted, grim smile that belies his usual cheerful expression.

"Ahhh… Eliza—it won't be long…not long now."

Leis softly recites the name of a deceased woman.

The next morning, in the labyrinth—

"So this is the door that leads to the boss room…"

Aria and company are standing near the labyrinth's center. A black stone slab is floating in the air in front of them…

It has a keyhole-shaped indentation in it, leading them to believe this is the entrance to the boss room, a door imbued with mana. Blue ripples pulsate ceaselessly from its center.

"Okay, Aria, if you put the key in the door, the path to the boss room will open!"

"I'm sure you guys will be fine, Aria, but please do take care!"

Lily and Feri call out to Aria and her party, having guided them here on the shortest possible path.

"Thank you for everything thus far, Lily and Feri."

"What are you talking about, Aria? We'll be right here waiting until you come back out."

"Yeah, we're so happy to become friends with you all. We want to stay with you forever!"

"Lily, Feri… Hee-hee, okay, I got it. I guess we better hurry up and take care of the boss inside, then. Okay, let's go, Tama and Stella!"

"Meown—!" *Roger that, master!*

"All the enemies so far have been chumps. I can't wait to finally let loose!"

Tama and Stella both respond to Aria positively—they're raring to go. Hearing their resolve, Aria nods and takes the key she discovered yesterday out from between her breasts. It's the exact same size as the keyhole before her. She inserts and turns it, resulting in a loud *clack*. The key disappears into thin air as a brightly lit path appears before them—a path that wasn't there before.

"So this leads to the boss room—?"

Hmm. I definitely sense a fearsome level of hostility that I haven't picked up from our enemies so far.

Aria shudders while Tama broods over the situation. The idea of a powerful enemy at the end of this path seems to be giving Stella a rush.

"Okay, Lily and Feri—see you later!"

Aria sounds confident as she bids farewell to the two fairies and accompanies Stella and Tama onto the path.

"Goh-hhhhhhh—!!"

A thunderous roar erupts. The trail that Aria and her party have taken is void of both trees and grass and leads to a mysterious chamber that is nothing but empty space.

A fifteen-foot-tall bipedal dragon monster with a massive tree for a body is reposed in slumber in the center. As Aria and her crew approach, the dragon opens its eyes and roars.

"I knew this drake would be extremely powerful! But we will not be afraid! Right, Stella?!"

"Yeah, I know! Hmph…!"

Aria falters for a moment in the face of the first treant drake she's ever seen, but she quickly gathers her wits and focuses, calling out to Stella, who is staring into the drake's maw.

Stella plants herself directly in front of the treant drake, hoisting her Mega Shield.

"Gohhh—!!"

Seeing Stella jump out before it, the monster has determined that she will be its first target. It slashes its massive claws in her direction.

Shrrrring—!

The treant drake's claws collide with Stella's Mega Shield, sending sparks flying. It's relatively low-level, but this is still a dragon-type monster they're contending with.

Stella has transformed into her dragonewt form. Even though she's also been restored thanks to the benefits of Tama's Divine Lion Protection, the force of impact sends her backward, albeit slightly.

However, Stella has not simply deflected the attack. She brandishes her greatsword in her other hand and brings it down against the beast's claws.

"Gohhh-bhhh—?!"

The treant drake screams in pain. Its claws have likely been damaged. Stella has attacked only once from a defensive position, but the drake's body is made of wood. Given Stella's power, landing a single blow is more than satisfactory.

"Meown—!" *Now!*

Tama races forward from Aria's feet at high speed. With the godlike speed he's gained from Divine Lion Protection, he slides around to the treant drake's flank while it's recoiling in pain.

"Meown—!" *Eat this! Flame Howl!*

Tama unleashes one of his Elemental Howls, Flame Howl, aiming for the monster's feet. His howl immediately emits a rush of flame that engulfs the treant drake's leg. It spins and rolls around, trying to put out the blaze, but its leg has been reduced to a hunk of ash in an instant. When the flames finally subside, its charred branch snaps with a shrill *crack*. All that thrashing has caused the treant drake's leg to break.

Whoosh—!

In that moment, Aria—who had been watching closely for an opening—rushes forward like a speeding bullet. She intends to strike the beast in the heart.

This could be bad. The treant drake realizes it's in extreme danger and lashes out at the elf with its undamaged claw.

"Meown—!" *Fat chance! Summon Tentacle!*

In the split second that their foe begins to move, Tama has already sprung into action. He activates Summon Tentacle and wraps up the treant drake's arm, throwing it off course and protecting his master.

Aria has sensed that Tama would protect her, and she doesn't falter, rushing the treant drake's chest.

And then—

Thisssp—!

Aria pierces the creature's chest with both her knives.

"Goh...ohhhhhhh...!"

The treant drake cries out in anguish.

The source of a dragon-type monster's life force is hidden in its chest. Aria was waiting for the perfect moment to pierce it.

Between Stella's defense, Tama's Elemental Howl acting as a distraction, and Aria going in for the kill the moment the treant drake was immobilized—everything went according to Aria's plans.

"Tama, Stella! We did it!"

The instant Aria confirms the light has left the boss's eyes, Aria cries out with joy.

"Meownnn—!" *Very well done, master!*

"Yay! Now I can eat some delicious food again!"

Tama is beyond pleased that Aria's battle plan was a success, and Stella goes wild imagining the huge feast she'll get to enjoy afterward.

"Tama, are you able to store the treant drake's corpse?"

"Meown—!" *No problem, master!*

Tama activates his Storage skill and stashes the entire husk inside.

"I—I can't believe you can store something so massive..."

A sheepish grin is stuck on Aria's face as she tries to comprehend the sheer volume that Tama can sock away with his Storage skill.

However, she quickly has a different reason to be surprised—in the spot from which the treant drake's corpse vanished, a beautifully adorned chest appears.

"A treasure box...and from the boss room... I wonder what could be inside?"

Aria opens the chest to find a rolled-up piece of sheepskin paper within.

"Huh, is this a scroll?"

"A ska-roll? Is it tasty?"

"Stella, a scroll is a magic item that grants its user a skill. This scroll is—huh, no use—it's written in ancient language. I have no idea what skill this scroll will grant."

"Meown?" *What?! A scroll inscribed with ancient language?! Master, you must use it for yourself!*

A shocked Tama tries to pantomime with his hands and feet (?) to communicate that Aria should definitely use the item. He does so because this parchment is inscribed with ancient letters, meaning the scroll itself could contain an "ancient skill."

There are different types of ancient skills, including low-level, mid-level, high-level, ultra-high-level, and above that, rare-level ancient skills that hardly anyone is able to wield. Furthermore, there are also innate ancient skills that have only a single user in the entire world.

The skill rankings above ultra-high-level almost always indicate extremely powerful abilities. If this scroll indeed bestows its user with an ancient skill, it will likely be a huge help to Aria, who still has reservations about her battle prowess.

"Tama, are you trying to say I should use it? But Stella might want to, or we could sell it..."

"Meow!" *Selling it would be an absolute waste, master!*

"Hmph. I have no need for new skills. Not to mention, I'm still hiding an ace up my sleeve! Aria, you are weak, so you should use it for yourself."

Stella seems to understand what Tama was trying to say and repeats it for Aria. Both she and Tama encourage her to put it to use.

Then Aria says:

"I understand. In that case, I will. Here goes... Activate scroll!"

The second Aria utters those words, the parchment turns to dust, and a dazzling light envelops Aria immediately.

"...! O-oh my gosh! It's an ancient skill, of all things! It's called 'Sacred Blade.' And its elemental attribute is... It's a holy elemental skill...?!"

"Meown!" *What?! A holy attribute?!*

After using the scroll, details regarding her newly acquired skill fill Aria's mind. She whispers, shocked at the information presented to her.

Tama is similarly bewildered.

The holy elemental distinction is an immensely powerful elemental attribute that dwells within individuals known as heroes who are strong enough to contend with a demon lord, or others with similarly formidable prowess.

Holy elemental attributes are well-known as the weak point of all monsters in existence. The same can be said for demons and demon lords.

If this elemental skill...this powerful brand of ancient skill has indeed been added to her repertoire, Aria and Tama have due reason to be shocked.

"Let's give it a try! Sacred Blade!"

Aria slashes the air with her knife, and a beam of silver-white light surges from her blade. Before she realizes it, the beam slices through the floor like butter.

In the moments after Aria activated the skill, a high-pitched sound resembling angelic singing fills the chamber...

"Th-the ground split in two...and it seems its range is about three feet. This skill is very formidable..."

Aria is further taken aback by the gift's fearsome power and its lightning-quick activation.

Hmm, this skill is truly powerful. This will supplement master's weak points—range and firepower—quite nicely. And the extended range during activation only means that my master's trademark tricky, speedy movement won't be adversely affected, either. It's not only an exceptional skill—it also complements her extremely well.

Tama nods deeply in satisfaction at the functionality of Sacred Blade.

"Here I am practicing my new skill, but we need to head back and meet up with Lily and Feri again!"

Aria wants to keep testing it out, but with Lily and Feri waiting for them outside, she decides to return to them posthaste.

"Huh? Lily? Feri?"

A perplexed voice escapes Aria shortly after the party exits the boss room. The fairy folk should have been waiting to greet them, but they're nowhere to be found.

"Lily! Feri! Where are you?"

Stella calls out the two girls' names loudly. She had fully planned on returning to Gladstone and tearing into a massive feast immediately.

However, neither girl appears, and they don't respond from afar, either.

"I wonder if something happened? Tama, Stella—we have to look for them!"

"Meown!" *Of course, master!*

"What a pain in the ass."

The three party members rush off to look for their new friends... but even after searching for several hours, they can't find the two girls.

Aria thought she heard a sound like a bell ringing in the

labyrinth, but she was so invested in looking for Lily and Feri that she didn't even realize what it was…

⟡

"We couldn't find them…"

"Meown…" *Master*…

As the party returns to Gladstone, Aria murmurs with sadness in her voice. Where could Lily and Feri possibly have gone…?

Stella also looks somewhat dejected.

"Oh? If it isn't Aria."

A voice rouses Aria and company from their despondence. They turn around to see several men and women standing there dressed in armor.

"Danny…? And everyone else, too… What are you doing here?"

The knight squadron from Labyrinthos has appeared, including all first squadron members—Danny, Howard, Keni, and Marietta. However, their captain, Cedric, is not present…

"We came to train with Gladstone's knight squadron."

"A few times a year, we conduct joint training with other cities."

Just as Danny and Howard said, the knight squadrons of Labyrinthos and Gladstone participated in joint training sessions semiannually.

"Our captain had important business, and he's off to a different city currently."

"He might be leading an ultra-top-secret mission, I suspect."

Watching Aria glance in every direction searching for Cedric, Keni and Marietta realize who she's looking for and tell her what's up.

"By the way, Aria, who's this beauty?"

"Ah, I haven't introduced you yet. This is Stella—she joined our party a while back."

"Oh, a new party member? Nice to meet you, Stella!"

Danny and his group get acquainted with Stella, who responds awkwardly.

"And that shield—is it the Mega Shield from Vulcan's workshop?"

"Come to think of it, Vulcan once told me that her friend Sakura used to wield this shield. Wasn't Sakura your old captain, Danny?"

"Yes, that's right. I really didn't think anyone would turn up who could hoist that stupid huge thing."

"Danny, it's about time."

"Ohhh, you're right, Howard; I almost forgot. Okay, Aria, we have to start practice now, so we'll be on our way."

"Okay, best of luck to all of you!"

Aria sees Danny and company off as they say their good-byes. She looks slightly more encouraged after running into friends.

"Huh? Looks like Leis's facility is closed today."

Aria and her companions have arrived in front of Leis's storehouse, intending to sell off the materials from the treant drake. However, the facility is closed.

"Oh well. Let's give up for now and head back to the inn."

The party could visit Gladstone's guild to sell their goods, but that would mean paying processing fees, which would be more trouble than it's worth. They decide to visit Leis again tomorrow.

"Excuse me, are you Aria?"

As Aria and company return to the inn, an elderly gentleman calls out to them. Judging from the tailcoat he's wearing, he must be a steward for an aristocratic family...

"Yes, I am..."

Aria responds reluctantly to the man in the tailcoat. And for good reason. This city's aristocracy only makes her think of the infamous earl she heard about from Joey.

"Hmm, very well. The lord of this city, the Earl of Gladstone, has summoned you to his estate. You shall follow me."

The steward is a servant of the earl after all. His face is expressionless as he commands Aria indifferently, obviously expecting her to obey without question.

It would seem that in such a short time, word of Aria's incomparable beauty has reached the earl.

As she glances around the inn, she realizes that all the patrons are looking at her sympathetically. They know the fate of those who catch the earl's eye.

Tama's face reads, *Like I would ever let my beloved master go with you!* as he glares at the steward.

"…?! You have no right of refusal. In this city, if you do not comply with the earl, you will be brought to justice as a criminal."

The steward is frightened by Tama's scowl but quickly recalls the earl's authority and becomes obstinate. Even in public, he's brazenly threatening to arrest Aria on false charges if she refuses.

"And you there—you're quite stunning as well. I'm sure the earl would like you, too. Come along."

"I don't know what you're saying, but I refuse."

Hearing the steward's demand to accompany him, Stella turns away with her usual haughty "hmph!"

Not too long ago, Stella would have been enraged at being told what to do and would likely have ended the steward's life on the spot. However, thanks to meeting Aria and the others, she has become much calmer. There's no concern of her recklessly attacking another person anymore.

"Stella, let's go with him."

"Meown—!" *Master?!*

Tama cries out in shock. Yet, seeing Aria's expression, he quickly thinks, *Oh, I see what you're up to!* and is convinced.

If Aria rejects the steward now, she will be tried on false charges. In that case, she plans to visit the earl of her own accord, see whether the rumors about him are true, and then bring him to justice in the name of righteousness when she finds an opening.

Aria is smart as a whip. The ace in the hole to make the plan succeed is Aria herself—and she knows it.

Tama now realizes what she's up to. He stops glaring at the steward and pretends to let Aria scoop him up peacefully.

"Very good. In that case, our carriage is waiting out front. Get in promptly."

Aria and her friends do as they're told.

Stella resists at first, but Aria promises her as much delicious food as she wants when it's all done, and she follows suit.

"Ooh! What incredible beauty! I've never seen such gorgeous ladies before in my life!"

Just minutes after bumping back and forth in the carriage, Aria and her crew arrive at the earl's estate and are led to a guest room. After waiting for a while, they hear a voice accompanied by a massive, ugly man with a face like a pig's. His gaudy robe is indicative of his overall poor taste.

This man could only be the Earl of Gladstone who has deprived so many individuals of happiness and defiled so many women.

"Pleased to make your acquaintance. I am an adventurer named Aria. This is my partner Tama and a member of our party, Stella."

Aria replies formally, for good measure. The earl nods in satisfaction and sits down heavily on a sofa with a tremendous *thud*. He silently appraises Aria from her breasts to her legs, like he's licking a plate clean, before turning to Stella sitting next to her and repeating the entire process.

"Forgive me, my lord—what business did you have with us when you requested our presence?"

"The answer is simple, Aria. You shall become my lover!"

"...I'm sorry, but that is not possi—"

A knock at the door interrupts Aria's refusal after she pauses for a moment at the demand she knew the earl would make.

"Pardon me. I've prepared us some tea."

With his head bowed low, the steward from before enters the room. He has a tea set in his left hand.

The steward skillfully pours tea while the earl watches with a smirk on his face.

"No matter, then. First, you should have some tea and relax. It's a luxurious brand that commoners can't acquire, you know?"

Aria assumed the earl would fly into a fit of rage at her refusal, but rather, he looks even more pleased than before and orders the girls to drink the refreshment provided by his servant.

It's almost as if…this was his plan all along.

This tea… Could it be poisoned?!

Aria has a realization, but she reaches out for her cup anyway and brings it to her lips.

She has an idea. The moment before she puts the tea to her lips, she whispers, "Tama, now."

Of course, Tama knows what to do. The instant the teacup touches Aria's mouth—

"Meown—!"

Tama cries out and activates Divine Lion Protection. Seeing Aria suddenly enveloped in sparkling golden light, the earl cries out, "What the—?!"

She pays him no attention and downs her cup with a smile.

"Hee-hee, that *is* good tea, my lord."

The earl's eyes grow even wider as Aria continues.

"Unfortunately for you, I've resisted the poison you laced it with thanks to Tama's skill. The drug contained an aphrodisiac and a hypnotic, right?"

Aria bores her gaze into the earl. Her hunch about the poisoned tea was correct, it seems. However, Tama's Divine Lion Protection means that all forms of poison are rendered null. What's more, thanks to the resistance, she's able to tell exactly what type of poison she's imbibed.

"Wh-what is the meaning of this?! I have not poisoned your tea whatsoever!"

"Is that so? Well then, why don't you try a sip yourself?"

"Wow…you're really doubting me, the earl? What insolence… Enough to throw you in jail for treason."

Aria is convinced: *We've cornered him now!*

However, the earl stays cool and feigns ignorance. If anything, he thinks he can throw Aria in jail for treason and claim her for himself. It's likely that, up until now, he's used his privilege to silence anyone who opposes him and to murder any witnesses, not leaving a shred of viable evidence of his many crimes.

"In that case, I'm afraid we'll have to rough you up a bit..."

Aria crouches down, ready to pounce.

"You swine! What do you think you're doing?! Do you think you can get away with laying a hand on me?!"

"It sounds like a stupid move, right? But not today—because we have an ace up our sleeve that will prove your crimes to the world."

With an ice-cold gaze, Aria speaks indifferently to the enraged earl.

In response, the aristocrat thinks, *This little bitch...*, and looks like he's just bitten down on a pernicious, bitter bug. He has no idea what the ace up Aria's sleeve could be. However, because she is so calm and collected in the face of his haughty threats, he realizes she could indeed have something on him to bring him down.

"So will you admit what you were planning to do? Or else...?"

"Shit...! Guards! Get them—!"

Backed into a corner by Aria, the earl is thrown into consternation. He quickly flies into a frenzy and calls out to his guards, likely waiting just outside the door, to sic them on Aria and company. In that moment...

"My lord, I have grave news—!"

The door to the room flies open with a bang and the earl's servant appears. He looks like he's seen a ghost.

"What the hell?! Now is not the time!"

"It's undead! An army of undead has suddenly appeared in the city center!"

"What did you say?! What on earth is going on?!"

The earl's reply reveals his obvious fear. Judging from his reaction, it doesn't seem to be a ploy to escape the corner into which he's been backed.

"Oh no! Tama, Stella, let's head to the city center at once!"

"Meown—!" *Of course, master!*

"I dunno what's happening, but it looks like I'll get to go berserk on some people!"

They have the earl's back against a wall, just where they want him, but if what's supposedly happening is true, that takes precedence. Aria and Tama, with their strong sense of righteousness, cannot ignore this plight.

Stella's interest is piqued, and for that reason, she joins them in flying from the earl's estate.

Clack-clack-clack-clack—

A horde of undead monsters—skeletons—swarms in the city center, giving off an inorganic rattle. Every one of them is holding a blade made from bones, which they use to slash down any humans they come across. It's a mess of blood, shrieking, and wailing—

—the city center of Gladstone has become a scene straight out of hell.

Clack-clack-clack-clack—!

The skeletons' bones clatter together like laughter while they swing their blades at the city's denizens. They're approaching a lone young girl.

She's frozen immobile and silent, crouching.

"Not on my watch!"

Just as a skeleton rears back to strike her—

A beam of light erupts in tandem with Aria's powerful voice, disintegrating the corpse into thin air without a sound.

Aria speaks reassuringly to the cowering girl. "It's okay now. But get out of here as fast as you can!"

The source of the beam came from Aria unleashing Sacred Blade.

"U-ummm… Thank you!"

The girl somehow manages to stand as she speaks and dashes off on shaky legs to an area void of skeletons.

"My goodness, this is an inordinate number of skeletons… But we have to protect the people of this city! I will focus on the undead attacking people. Tama, support me, and, Stella…go wild!!"

"Meown!" *Understood, master!*

"Gah-ha-ha-ha! Now you're speaking my language!"

Faced with a veritable sea of skeletons, Aria provides instruction to Tama and Stella, respectively. In reality, she wishes she could use Stella as a tank to slowly and surely whittle away at the skeletons' numbers, but right now the creatures are attacking the residents in succession.

For the moment, they need to cull their opponents' ranks, and quickly, as opposed to prioritizing the safest fighting position. It's extremely fortunate that Aria just acquired her holy elemental skill, Sacred Blade.

Skeletons are weak to fire elemental, holy elemental, and blunt attack damage. They are now Aria's prey.

"Sacred Blade—!!"

Aria unleashes her new skill again on a skeleton bearing down on a bystander. The silver-white beam of light blasts the undead's head off, and in the same moment, another skeleton raises its blade to slash Aria from behind. She realizes this but remains focused on another target in front of her.

Aria has faith.

She believes that Tama, her beloved pet (knight), will protect her.

"Meown!" *No way you'll hurt my master!*

Just as Aria expects, the little cat quickly jumps into action. He howls adorably, and his equally adorable tail burns a bright, deep crimson.

A pillar of flame immediately rushes from his tail with a

ferocious *whoosh*, converging on the skeleton that attempted to attack Aria's rear. It's a veritable longsword made of fire.

Shrrring—!

The blade of flame rips the undead in half from the skull downward. In the same moment, Aria obliterates the skeleton in front of her.

"T-Tama... Did you also have a close-range attack skill?"

"Meowr—!"

Aria is shocked that her pet would display another new skill at this juncture, but Tama simply replies with a cute little mew.

He'd activated one of his innate skills—an Elemental Tail Blade—called Flame Edge. Tama determined that using skills like Summon Tentacle to support his master would be insufficient to protect the city. To this end, in order to drive down the number of skeletons, he decided to reveal the close-range attack skill he'd been hiding.

In terms of obliterating the enemies' ranks, the best choice would be the Elemental Howl Flame Howl—given its superior range and span—however, because of the people and buildings nearby, he can't use a skill that could cause a fire.

"Could it be?! That is the flame blade that defeated me in one fell swoop. I won't let you beat me again!"

Seeing Tama activate the ability used to defeat her with a single attack in her previous life as an earth dragon, Stella is more eager than ever to jump into battle. She rushes into an area flush with skeletons for an ambush, using her Mega Shield and greatsword in tandem to blast through droves of foes with ease.

As stated earlier, skeletons are weak to blunt damage attacks. Stella's shield-bash yields instantaneous success, and attacks from her greatsword—which is really more geared toward smashing than slashing—are equally effective.

"Look! The adventurers are fighting! All reinforcements on deck!!"

""""Yessir—!!""""

As Aria and company manage to decimate the skeletons' forces, a powerful voice resounds through the city center.

"Danny!"

Wiping sweat from her brow, Aria's expression instantly lights up. Danny stands before her, along with Howard, Keni, Marietta, and what appears to be a gathering of troops from the Gladstone knight squadron.

At Danny's command, the knights rush in unison toward the undead horde.

"Geh-hya-hya-hya! Attack all you want—it's no use!"

Howard bashes through skeletons with his shield and deflects attacks to protect his comrades.

"Sheesh, skeletons are a real pain in the ass!"

Danny steps in with his sword to deftly block the attacks that Howard can't deflect himself, driving the skeletons back. Slash attacks aren't supposed to be effective against skeletons, but a single swipe reduces them to a heap of bones.

"Oi! I'll slice you to bits!"

"I'll pulverize you!"

Keni and Marietta swoop in from the flank for a sneak attack on some stragglers that have let their guard down. Keni takes advantage of the weight of her battle-ax and aims for the skeletons' joints as she brings them down. Marietta uses her *bo* to smash their skulls.

This squadron is filled with proper troops after all. The skeletons are driven back, one by one.

"We may not be knights, but we're here to help, too!"

Several more voices echo from another direction.

"No one asked us to be here, but if the city is destroyed, we'll lose our jobs! Let's go!"

The group rushes toward the invaders. It's Joey—he's arrived with his comrades as reinforcements.

Joey and his crew are skilled adventurers. They aren't exactly on par with the knight squadron, but through their combined efforts, they make quick work of the skeletons and reduce their numbers.

We might just have a shot…!

Aria is now convinced, thanks to the reinforcements.

Just as she drinks down a potion to restore her mana, Aria hears someone saying, "This is less than ideal. If everything had gone according to plan, by now, all the people in the city center would be dead, and we'd be storming the earl's estate…"

Looking toward the source of the voice, she realizes it's coming from Leis's company storehouse. Leis stands in the doorway, his eyes burning with rage.

"Leis…is that you? What are…? Wait, why are they with you?!"

Aria's eyes grow wide in shock as she addresses Leis. Lily and Feri are paralyzed at his feet, their eyes blank and vacant.

"They are under the control of my magic item. I call it the Spirit Slave Bell…"

Leis holds the item in his left hand, showing it to Aria—it's a small bell that emits a chime. Pale ripples emanate from Lily's and Feri's bodies in sync with the sound.

"That noise… And Lily and Feri don't look right… Leis, you kidnapped them in the labyrinth, didn't you?! Just what do you plan on doing with them?!"

"Heh-heh… That's exactly right, Aria. I was the one who abducted them. My plan is…this!"

Aria then realizes that the chime she heard in the forest labyrinth was the sound of Leis's Spirit Slave Bell.

Leis smiles menacingly, and this time, he raises his right hand, showing the arrow-shaped item he's holding.

""Ahhhhhhhh—!!""

When Leis holds up the arrow, Lily and Feri scream in pain. At the same time, beams of light fly from their bodies and gather into the magic item.

"What are you doing?! Stop it right now!"

"Meowrn—!" *You heathen!*

Aria and Tama don't know what he's doing, but it's obvious Leis has paralyzed Lily and Feri and is causing them pain. That's all the reason they'd ever need to spring into action.

"Create Skeleton!"

As Aria and Tama move to attack, Leis yells out an attack of his own, and a flash of purple light erupts in front of them. Just as the light dissipates, a number of skeletons appear in the same location.

"Summoning the undead? Leis, are you a necromancer?"

"Very astute of you, Aria. I have skills that can create undead beings. I will use them to destroy this city and get my revenge on the earl—!!"

Spittle flies from Leis's mouth as he screams with rage, his eyes bulging wide.

Revenge... So that's what this is about.

Tama remembers the story Joey told them—about Leis's fiancée being defiled at the hand of the earl and coming back to him as a corpse—

Leis intends to take everything from the earl by destroying his city. Just like his fiancée, who he loved, was taken from him...

"I wasn't able to have my revenge until now because the mana I held was simply too weak. I could only summon two skeletons at most. But thanks to these fairies, I was able to acquire a vast amount of mana...!"

Releasing years of pent-up rage, Leis dispatches more skeletons to attack Aria and Tama.

Leis kidnapped Lily and Feri as part of his plot to exact vengeance. Fairies contain massive amounts of mana. To acquire it, Leis subdued them with the Spirit Slave Bell, and using the magic item in his right hand—the Mana Drain Arrow—he was able to absorb their mana.

"Fairies have the most incredible mana—as you can see, I was able to summon enough skeletons to raze this city to the ground!"

Leis's tone is completely different. In that moment, Stella reconvenes with Aria and Tama to regain her stamina after rampaging against the skeleton army.

All around them, the knight squadron and the party of adventurers are engaged in battle with the remnants of the undead.

"All that said, your plan will end in futility. We are going to stop it—just watch!"

Aria points her knives at Leis with a bold challenge before dashing off toward the group of skeletons he just summoned.

"Hmph! Just when I thought I'd take a breather!"

Seeing Aria rush off, Stella runs up behind her.

"Sacred Blade—!"

Aria brings down her blade of light against the undead blocking her path. Three of their bodies are sliced completely in half as they crumble.

Whroosh—

A number of new skeletons crowd in to replace the ones that have been blown apart. The first lashes out with its sword to pierce Aria.

"No chance!"

With her Mega Shield in one hand, Stella springs out in front of the elf, whose knife remains pointed downward from her previous slash. Stella's transformed into her dragonewt form, and a skeleton's swordplay is useless against her.

She charges forward with her Mega Shield and bashes into a number of its brethren at once, sending them flying.

"Meown—!" *Don't even think of touching my master!*

Now that Stella's in the vanguard, it's Tama's turn to show his might. As Stella mows down one group of skeletons, others keep attacking in succession. Although Aria's Sacred Blade is strong, she can't quite deal with this many enemies at once.

In order to protect her, Tama unleashes Flame Edge and burns through the approaching minions.

Grrr... I can't deal with this many, either, even with Flame Edge...
In that case—

Even Tama's Flame Edge isn't putting a dent in the enemy's vast numbers. That means Tama will need to unleash a different skill. While attacking with Flame Edge, he slashes with his front paws.

In the next moment...

Slash—!

A skeleton crumbles to bits as a piercing sound rings out. The tiny behemoth has unleashed his newly acquired skill Dragon Claw. An invisible claw appears out of thin air and rips through the skeleton, shattering it completely.

Stella continues blocking with her Mega Shield and obliterating enemies with her greatsword. Aiming for gaps in the skeletons' movements created thanks to Stella, Aria begins to unleash Sacred Blade again.

Activating his behemoth skills and relying on his competency as a knight in a previous life, Tama supports them both perfectly.

"*Pant, pant...* Leis! This is the end of the line!"

Over ten minutes later, Aria levels the tip of her knife at Leis again, having managed to clean up the skeletons with Tama and Stella. She's breathing heavily, her shoulders heaving, expression strained.

Sacred Blade boasts a powerful fiery beam of light, but using it requires a large amount of mana. Having unleashed it over five times to successfully drive back all the skeletons, Aria's mana is almost wholly depleted.

However, that shouldn't be a problem given current circumstances. Leis no longer has a wall to protect him... At least, that's what Aria thinks.

Hearing the elf, Leis responds, "Unfortunately, that won't be happening. I have an ace up my sleeve...!"

Leis holds both his hands to the sky. In that moment—
Dwo-goooooooooooon—!

An explosion erupts and Leis's company storehouse is blown away. A massive, hulking figure appears in its place.

"What the…?!"

"Meow!" *It's the earth dragon skeleton!*

"You bastard! You think you can manipulate my body?!"

Aria and Tama cry out in surprise. The gargantuan figure is the skeleton of the earth dragon they were tasked with escorting safely to Gladstone.

However, it's obvious it's no longer just a regular skeleton. It seems practically alive, and black miasma emanates from its enormous form. The same obsidian fog is also pouring from Leis's body.

Just as Stella said, Leis is now manipulating the skeleton of an S-ranked monster—an earth dragon.

"Now! After them! Earth dragon—no, undead dragon! Death to anyone who stands in the way of my revenge!"

Gwo-ooooooooooooh—!

In response to Leis's call, the earth dragon skeleton—now an undead dragon—roars viciously.

"Urgh…!"

Aria is paralyzed with fear. That much should be obvious, given the vicious roar that tore through the atmosphere and shook her to the core—a roar of the first S-ranked monster she's ever confronted.

However, Aria is still bestowed with the power of Tama's Divine Lion Protection, which also gives its target increased resistance against fear.

Aria feels paralyzed for a moment, but her heart quickly ignites with a sense of confidence, and she looks at the undead dragon with resolute fortitude.

"Meow?" *Master, are you going to fight it?*

A cry involuntarily escapes Tama as he watches Aria stare down her enemy.

Aria gives Tama a slight nod in response.

"It might only be my body from a past life, but I'll put you to certain death for manipulating it!"

Stella cries out gruffly as she hoists her greatsword. She's clearly furious that her remains are being so blatantly abused. Blue veins pop from her forehead.

"I don't know what it is, but this thing is terrifying! Half the squadron—focus on attacking! The remaining half—fall back to evacuate the citizens!"

Seeing the undead dragon appear, Danny gives the knights orders. Joey also deploys his adventurer comrades.

"I won't let you touch it! Create Skeleton!"

Leis screams, and as the adventurers and knights both rush toward Aria and company to lend their assistance, another horde of undead appears before them.

Grrr... I don't know how much fighting this body of mine has in it, but I'll give this all I have!

Tama readies his Flame Edge and bores his gaze into the undead dragon—an S-rank monster resurrected. Last time he faced the earth dragon, Tama was able to defeat it because he evolved to his next form. However, the words *Evolution Possible: Behemoth (second form)* no longer appear on his status display.

How far will he get in battle without evolving...?

Gwo-ooooooh—!

The undead dragon lashes out with its front claws, and Aria and Tama both jump back to avoid them. But Stella doesn't move.

"Wrhoooooooaoh—!"

Stella screams and holds her Mega Shield over her head.

Zzzrrring—!

The undead dragon's claws collide dramatically with her Mega Shield.

Stella has already changed into her dragonewt form. She thought she would show the undead dragon that she can withstand its attacks, but in that moment—

Leis holds the Mana Drain Arrow high and screams, "Mana, enter the undead dragon now!" A plume of black miasma erupts from the arrow and is absorbed into the undead dragon's body, turning it a shade darker.

"Grrrr?!"

Stella cries out awkwardly. The beast has clearly gained a measure of additional power from the mana Leis granted it. Stella is unable to withstand the pressure and swings her Mega Shield to the side, escaping from the undead dragon's front claws.

"Stella couldn't hold it back?! This S-ranked undead monster is truly something else…!"

Seeing Stella overpowered, Aria cries out in shock. Meanwhile, Tama is already on to his next move.

"Meown!!"

Tama gives a brief mew and rushes directly toward the undead dragon. Its reaction is delayed from exerting energy after trying to crush Stella, giving the little behemoth an opportunity to close in on it.

Tama pushes his Flame Edge into the dragon's chest and rushes even farther forward.

"You goddamn elemental cat! You're after me, aren't you?"

Leis realizes what Tama is doing—he intends to attack the necromancer Leis at the same time he deals damage to the undead dragon.

"Do you really think I'll allow that? Undead dragon, finish off this elemental cat now!"

Gwo-oooooh—!

The undead puppet replies to Leis with a vicious roar and uses its powerful tail to lash out at Tama, now beneath its chest.

"Meown!!" *Oh shit!*

Tama takes a massive sidestep to avoid the undead dragon's tail attack, but he's too late—the tip of the tail grazes him.

"Tama…!!"

Aria screams, rife with worry—Tama was thrown with considerable force.

"Meown—!" *Don't worry, master!*

Tama pays Aria's concern no mind and sticks a perfect landing while mewing nonchalantly.

The second before Tama received the tail attack, he activated the Iron Body skill he previously acquired from a golem in the labyrinth, causing his body to become rigid and protect him.

But that isn't all he's got. As he lands, Tama activates Summon Tentacle.

Whoooosh—

Two tentacles fly out from beneath Tama's feet and slip through the undead dragon's legs, reaching Lily and Feri. The tentacles instantly wrap around the two fairies and pull them toward Tama.

"Shit! He's taken the fairies!"

Leis curses in vexation.

Hmph, it seems like I was right all along.

Seeing Leis's reaction, Tama is convinced of one thing.

Why is Leis keeping Lily and Feri so close to him, even though they'll surely be endangered?

Tama guesses it's because there's a certain range of effect necessary to absorb mana from them with the Mana Drain Arrow.

Of course, Tama has other reasons. He wanted to save them as quickly as possible, knowing that Leis would try to kidnap them again when the tables turned.

Tama uses his tentacles to set Lily and Feri down somewhere safe.

"Nice one, Tama! Now we don't need to hold back!"

"Meown!"

With Lily and Feri's safety in mind, Tama had also been hesitant to unleash his full fury. Now there isn't a lick of worry.

"Let's go!"

Aria rushes forward.

She activates her skill Acceleration, combined with Divine Lion

Protection bestowed on her by Tama, and reaches top speed in an instant, closing the gap between her and the undead dragon's legs like a speeding bullet.

"Kill her! Crush her dead!"

Leis shows no mercy as he shouts orders at the dragon. His complete change in disposition belies the friendly way he interacted with Aria during their quest.

He clearly had his guard up the entire time.

"Meown—!" *No way!*

The undead dragon slashes at Aria with its front claws, but Tama activates Summon Tentacle again to trap its legs. It's not enough to completely rob the S-ranked monster of its strength, but Tama is successful in altering the course of its attack.

Aria twists her body in the air and displays a risky, superhuman flip to land directly on the creature's front legs.

"Sacred Blade—!!"

A silver-white beam erupts—Aria's blade of light extending from her knife bores into the enemy's forelegs.

Aria puts every last ounce of her mana into this single attack.

Gwo-ooooooh—!

The dragon roars, this time sounding like it's in agony.

Every monster in existence is weak to holy elemental attacks, and they're especially effective against undead monsters. An ancient skill imbued with the holy elemental attribute is enough to elicit an anguished shriek from even an undead dragon.

"Tama, Stella, it's time to finish it off! We'll only have one chance…!"

"Meown—!!" *Understood, master!*

"It's time to pull the ace out! Tama and Aria, I need you to give it your all!"

Tama and Stella are quick to indicate their readiness.

At this juncture, Aria and her party are working together

almost effortlessly. Even without detailed explanation, each member understands what they should be doing.

"Get ready! Dragonic Power—Full Drive!!"

Stella roars, and her dragon-form arms audibly swell and emit a faint glow.

"Rarrrwwwohhhhhhhh—!!"

Stella rushes toward the enemy in the blink of an eye—incomparable to any speed she's displayed thus far.

The creature flips over and lashes out with a horizontal tail sweep. Stella looks like she'll get sideswiped and blasted sideways—and all the knights and adventurers gather as much.

However—

"Gwo-ahhhhhhhhhhh?!"

The undead dragon's roar is tinged with surprise, and rightfully so—Stella used her Mega Shield for a charge attack that forcefully blasted its tail sweep back.

Stella's innate skill, Dragonic Power—Full Drive, is something she acquired when she reincarnated. It grants a five-times boost to the physical strength of her entire body when she's in dragonewt form.

As a proud dragon being, Stella hasn't yet revealed her most powerful abilities. But now she's up against her former self.

Only Stella can understand this enemy's true power, and she was compelled to demonstrate her hidden strength, the anger arising from seeing her body used for ill-gotten gains goading her.

The creature begins losing its balance—

Now!

—and using the opening that created, Aria grabs a potion from her garter belt and chugs it down before rushing forward.

Tama follows suit and charges toward Leis.

"Come, undead dragon!!"

Leis swings his right arm through the air in an attempt to

manipulate the beast. In response, even unbalanced, the puppet twists its body and slashes at Tama and Aria.

"Meown—!" *This is it!*

Just as the enemy's claws approach them, Tama swings his tail of flame and slices through the air.

Shrrrrrring—!!

A powerful, shrill blast accompanies the undead dragon's right-front leg being cleaved in half.

This is Tama's third time facing this enemy, including the two times he fought Stella before her reincarnation. Even though the earth dragon is now undead, its general move set has barely changed.

Tama is a storied warrior, and he sees through the beast's movements to cleave its leg clean off.

Aria is flabbergasted by Tama's superhuman swordsmanship maneuver but remains focused as she runs toward Leis.

"C-Create Skeleton!"

His voice panicked, Leis summons a group of ten skeletons as a shield.

"Sacred Blade—!!"

Aria doesn't hesitate, reaching Leis without dropping her speed and ripping through every last skeleton trying to stop her with a single horizontal beam of light. Aria sensed that Leis still had the power required to summon additional undead, and immediately before, she drank a potion that restored just enough mana to activate Sacred Blade one more time.

The skeletons hit with the holy elemental blade strike turn to dust before they can emit a single sound.

"You're finished, Leis."

Aria leaps over the lifeless skeletons and unleashes a jump kick at Leis. He might be a powerful necromancer, but in terms of physical strength, he's nothing more than an average man—he has no technique to avoid Aria's kick, which has been buffed by both Acceleration and Divine Lion Protection. The impact rocks him to the side, where he crumples on the ground in a heap, incapacitated.

"Dogwohhhhhhhhhh..."

A thunderous roar erupts from behind Aria. Whipping around, she sees that the undead dragon is falling apart.

"What the—?"

"The skeletons have stopped moving, too!"

Danny and Joey cry out from behind the undead dragon. Just like they said, the earth dragon is crumbling into a pile of bones.

Hmm, it appears the creature lost all its power when Leis, the one controlling it, fell unconscious.

Tama realizes what's going on.

Aria approaches the incapacitated Leis and says, "I will not allow you to do anything like this ever again."

She proceeds to rip the two magic items out of both his hands before throwing them high in the air and destroying them with Sacred Blade. This prevents Lily and Feri from being further controlled by him, and he can no longer absorb their mana.

"Okay—first order of business is to nurse Lily and Feri back to health, along with anyone else who was injured during this struggle."

Aria is exhausted from the fierce battle but asserts her intention to help anyone injured and begins doing so.

Stella is resting with her eyes closed as she recovers from unleashing her secret attack.

Tama has summoned tentacles to bind Leis in place, making sure he can't escape even if he wakes up.

Lily and Feri, who everyone was worried about, are still unconscious, but they don't appear mortally wounded. Realizing this, Aria sighs in relief.

In that moment—a voice reverberates throughout the city center.

"Come now, what are you waiting for?! This man is the master-mind behind this whole ordeal, right? Kill him already!"

It's the Earl of Gladstone, accompanied by his steward and a number of guards. He must have realized the coast was clear as he comes out from behind his entourage and goes to kick Leis's unconscious body.

Aria approaches the earl without a word and sweep kicks his feet out from under him, throwing him to the ground.

"Gyahhh—!"

"My lord!"

The earl cries out grotesquely, and his steward and guards rush to surround him.

"A-Aria, that probably wasn't very smart..."

Watching Aria, Danny makes a candid observation. No matter how obviously guilty the earl is, a commoner injuring a member of the aristocracy will not go unpunished.

Danny rushes to restrain the elf, even if only to make a show of it, before the earl can set his guards on her in a fit of psychotic rage... However...

"Danny. Please listen. You see..."

"What...? Aria, is that really true? Okay—Keni, Marietta! Restrain the earl immediately!"

"Wha—?! Just what are you doing?! I am the lord of this domain, the Earl of Gladstone!"

Aria whispers into Danny's ear, and Danny quickly orders his reluctant subordinates to seize the earl. He screams furiously at Danny and not Aria—who caused him harm—but it's no use.

"I'm sorry, but we are knights of the Marquis Estate. Defying our orders is equivalent to defying the House of Marquis. Further, our captain is the eldest son of the Marquis family, the hero captain Cedric Ruiné. For your own benefit, I suggest you comply with our orders."

"Gah...! The Marquis Estate?!"

Hearing *"Marquis Estate"*—the lords of Labyrinthos—and the family son's name, *"Cedric,"* the earl's face turns white as a sheet.

They are both aristocrat families, but the Marquis Estate outranks the Earl of Gladstone. Just as Danny said, his comrades comprise the number one knight squadron of the Marquis Estate. Defying their orders is tantamount to defying the Marquis.

The earl looks sickened but cooperates with Danny and the others' orders.

"Now then, Earl, it's time for you to get some sleep..."

"Gwa? Just what on earth are you—"

—*talking about?* the earl starts to say but loses consciousness before he has the chance. A strike to the neck from Danny puts him out instantly.

Of course, the earl's steward and guards—as well as the other knights and adventurers—are shocked by this continuation of violence that started with Aria.

"Aria! Let's give the earl a drink of that stuff you mentioned earlier."

"Thank you, Danny. This is it—the Teardrops of Truth."

Aria takes a small, glowing bottle out from her breast—the Teardrops of Truth that she acquired from the treasure box in the labyrinth.

When she told Danny exactly what atrocious acts the earl has committed, she also told him that she possesses this rare elixir.

Danny had also heard foul rumors of the earl. To test their validity and bring the earl to justice if necessary, he asked Aria for her help. After taking the Teardrops of Truth from Aria, he brings the vial to the earl's lips.

Howard, Keni, and Marietta block off the earl's guards, who attempt to stop the procedure, refusing to let them interrupt. Both the guards and the earl's steward turn white as ghosts.

The earl proceeds to reveal every last detail during Aria and

Danny's interrogation, though not of his own volition, and to confess all his sins.

"Wooow! This is so incredibly sweet!"

"This honey-preserved fruit is amazing, too!"

A few days later, two girls can be found at the bar in Gladstone, stuffing their cheeks with sweets, looking happy as can be—of course, it's Lily and Feri. The two of them were severely weakened after Leis stole their mana but today have fully recovered at last.

In celebration, Aria is treating them to as many of their favorite delicious sweets as they want.

The last few days have been filled with adventure.

Leis was apprehended by the city's knights for his actions. However, once it came to light during his interrogation that his fiancée had been captured and murdered by the earl, the extenuating circumstances spared him from being put to death. Instead, Leis was sentenced to life imprisonment for his crimes.

Now that the earl's numerous atrocities were out in the open, he was stripped of his status and sentenced to prison for the rest of his life, just like Leis.

Apparently, Leis looked extremely contented when informed of this in his cell…

"*Munch, munch!* Meat is the best food, after all!"

Next to Lily and Feri, Stella holds a huge bone-in chunk of meat in one hand, stuffing her cheeks like it's her last meal on earth. And next to her…

"Okay, Tama, open wide—!"

"Meown—!"

Aria pushes a forkful of food toward Tama's mouth to feed him.

"N-no fair! Let me feed Tama!"

"Yeah, I wanna feed Tama, too!"

"Me three!"

Watching Aria and Tama rubbing and loving on each other, Stella, Lily, and Feri all gather around them, shouting, "Not fair! Not fair! Not fair!"

Aria pays them no mind and squeezes Tama between her breasts as she strokes him lovingly.

Mmmm. We had some close calls, but I am very glad I was able to protect my master. I mustn't let my pride get the best of me, though. If my master continues on the path of righteousness, there will certainly be more battles to come!

Even as Aria gets rather touchy-feely with the affectionate petting, Tama reaffirms his knight's pledge to himself.

The adventures of the elf girl seeking justice and her chivalrous cat (behemoth) have only just begun.

"Meownnn…!"

The day before departing for Renald to collect the earth dragon corpse—Stella's previous form—Tama stretches contentedly as he awakens in a room of the inn in Labyrinthos.

Hmm, my master and the others are still asleep. I should get up and groom myself.

It's morning—Aria and Stella are sleeping peacefully next to Tama as he begins his daily grooming ritual.

He licks his front legs and paws to get himself clean all over. Even in his past life, Tama took great care with his appearance.

He washed his face every morning and tidied up his long silver locks (whose beauty his partner at the time was very jealous of) and tended to his silver armor before heading out to work.

Even now that he's been reincarnated as a behemoth…or rather, a behemoth cub who looks like a kitten, he still has the same preference regarding his self-grooming habits. Furthermore, even though Tama was once human, he has no qualms about licking his fur clean thanks to his feline instincts.

Okay, I'm done cleaning up. Time to wake master.

Tama makes his way over to Aria after he finishes his feline grooming diligence. He goes in to rub his face against her cheek while she sleeps, breathing quietly—however...

Master's face is so lovely, no matter how many times I see it... She's truly an angel...

Reflexively, Tama swallows a lump in his throat, astounded by Aria's beatific, sleeping face. Even though he should be used to it by now, when he lets down his guard, he is still captivated by her appearance.

Aria's looks are a truly miraculous combination of sweet and gorgeous. Tama has never seen a girl as fetching as her.

Oh no. As my master's knight, I must not allow myself to be this captivated by her.

Tama quickly manages to return to his senses. As Aria's knight and protector, for him to gaze transfixed upon his master's sleeping face would be inexcusable.

Tama uses his chivalry to rein himself in and takes a deep breath, then proceeds to rub his face against Aria's cheek to wake her.

"Mmmm... Good morning, Tama... You woke me up again today, huh...? ♡"

Aria's eyes open after Tama rubs his head on her cheek a few times, and she calls his name lovingly.

Aria adores Tama, and being woken by him is the happiest moment of her day. She pulls Tama closer and hugs him to her ample bosom.

My master is always rather heavy-handed with the touching... Yet obeying her desires is my duty as a knight. I cannot refuse.

Tama makes excuses in his own mind and slides between Aria's breasts.

"Awww... Tama, you are so darn cute... I really want you to grow up so we can *meow* together all night, but I really love fawning over you when you're so tiny like this, too..."

Aria still mistakenly thinks that Tama is an elemental cat, a kind of magical beast with which she can crossbreed. She's always thinking about how she one day wants to bear his child.

That said, the fact remains that Tama's cub form is unbearably cute and lovable as is. Aria is conflicted—she loves him as a kitten but also wants him to grow up so she can have her way with him.

She's still a young woman, but she can be lustful beyond her years.

"Meown—" *Mmmm, wow, master's touch is as incredible as always...*

Aria rubs Tama's head as she clutches his tiny body. It feels so good, and Tama cries out despite himself. She feels so soft, her touch is so adoring, and the sweet scent she gives off in close quarters envelops Tama in her motherly affection... There is no way the cub Tama can resist reciprocating like a child.

"Mmmm..."

Shortly after Aria starts fawning on Tama, Stella's voice can be heard from the next bed. She's awake.

"Good morning, Stella."

"...Hmph! N-no fair, you're holding Tama again!"

Stella yells out—even though she just woke up—when she sees Aria hugging Tama against her breasts.

—*Stella, lower your voice. You'll disturb the people next door.*

—*Grrr... I don't get it, but if you say so, Tama, I have no choice but to be quiet...*

Stella obediently complies with Tama's telepathic command.

"......?"

Aria looks perplexed as Stella quickly falls silent with a perturbed expression.

"Fine. At any rate, Stella, let's wash our faces and go get some breakfast."

"...! Okay! I love washing my face! And I love breakfast!"

Stella's face lights up in an instant. She is obsessed with eating, and she's grown fond of washing her face—well, really her whole body. When she was an earth dragon, she either lazed about or lost herself in the joy of crushing feeble enemies—that's it.

However, after meeting Aria and everyone else, Stella had her first bathing experience and now understands the comfort of cleaning her body. She heads straight for the sink in their room and twists the faucet, washing her face vigorously.

"Stella, no, no—you're a girl, right? You have to wash your face more gently..."

"Mm...? It feels good to wash your face with gusto!"

As Stella furiously scrubs, Aria explains how to wash up properly, but Stella doesn't get it.

"Stella. Girls need to take good care of their skin. Tama, you like girls with beautiful, healthy skin, right?"

"Meown—!"

"Mmmph! In that case, I will wash gently! I am a girl who knows how to take care of her skin!"

Seeing Tama's reaction to Aria's words, Stella starts washing her face gently. She was an S-ranked monster in a past life, but in Tama's presence, she's a lovestruck young woman.

"Good girl, Stella. You have to make sure to dry your face with a towel gently, too, okay?"

"Got it! I will dry my face with care!"

As instructed, Stella gently wipes the water from her face.

Seeing this, Tama is impressed as he thinks, *Wow, master can be very fastidious...*

"Okay, now it's time to change our clothes!"

"Right! And once we change, we can eat!"

Stella instantly throws off the negligee that Vulcan bought her. She's desperate for some breakfast.

Aria chuckles as she watches. Stella still has a long way to go in acting ladylike.

Aria comes close to cautioning her about this, too, but...in the end, she gives up, realizing that chiding Stella about every little thing and trying to rein her in too much will only cause her stress.

As long as she gets used to society bit by bit, right?

Aria looks at Stella fondly and starts changing herself.

Whoosh—Aria silently takes off her stark white negligee.

Neither Stella nor Aria wears a bra when they're sleeping. Aria has nothing but a black thong on now, and the sunlight through the window casts a warm glow on her body.

Her porcelain-white skin is flawless, and her platinum-blond hair falls down to her waist, her semitransparent ice-blue eyes shining like precious gems.

"Meown—!" *So gorgeous...*

Before Tama's thoughts can even edge into seedy territory, he is utterly fascinated by Aria's excessive level of fairy-tale-like beauty.

Ahhh... Tama's giving me that look... ♡

Aria's cheeks flush pink. She gets excited simply from her beloved Tama's attention. She brushes her private parts over the top of her ultra-tiny panties.

...I'm...definitely going to need to change my panties now...

Aria is much more aroused than she realized... By the time she finishes breakfast, her body will be flushed, and she'll be dripping with "honey."

She decides to return to her room and change her underwear.

"Okay, Tama, come here."

"Meown—!"

Even though she's aroused, Aria has finally managed to don her bikini armor, and as she opens her arms, Tama jumps up onto her chest.

Boi-oi-oing—

As she catches Tama, Aria's chest bounces up and down, looking so pillowy soft. Of course, Tama leaped into her arms with the utmost care in order to not hurt Aria's chest at all.

"Grrr! I want to hold Tama, too!"

Seeing Tama comfortably ensconced in between Aria's breasts, Stella is already grinding her teeth.

"Well, if it isn't Aria, Stella, and Tama! You guys are early again today!"

"Good morning! We're thinking about heading out on a quest again."

"Meown—!"

The proprietress of the inn greets the party at the first-floor restaurant. There isn't a single customer yet. Aria and her room-mates are the early birds.

"Mmmm...! That smells so good!"

Stella is so entranced by the delicious smell wafting from the kitchen, she doesn't even realize the proprietress has greeted them. She sniffs the air repeatedly as drool dangles from the corner of her mouth.

"Ha-ha! Stella, you're just like a little kid. Eat as much as you want again today!"

"I'm going to eat a ton! The *cuisine* here is delicious!"

The proprietress greets Stella with a laugh at the young woman's childish bearing, and Stella doubles down. Seeing this, Tama can't help but chuckle.

Aria says, "Stella, you learned a new word!" praising her like a mother for using *"cuisine."*

"Okay, I'll bring out the *cuisine* now, so just wait a minute."

The proprietress heads back into the kitchen.

"I can't wait to see today's *cuisine*! When I lived in the labyrinth, I had to catch my own prey for food, so this place is like a dream!"

"*'Your own prey'*—?! Oh my, Stella, did you eat monsters in the labyrinth?"

Aria looks totally shocked by this revelation about Stella, already holding a fork and knife, her eyes surging with excitement.

Confounded by the obvious nature of the question, the former earth dragon replies, "Of course I did! Wyvern meat is the tastiest!"

"Stella... From here on out, I'll feed you even more delicious food, okay...?"

Hearing how rough her friend had it in the past, Aria promises to feed Stella the best food possible, tears welling in her eyes. They are planning to leave on the merchant Leis's quest the next day, but Aria has no particular intention of taking it easy. Starting tomorrow, she won't be able to delve into the labyrinth for a while, and she's worried she'll get rusty.

That's why Aria wants to accept a quest today, too. The other reason is because Stella's rampage meant that she didn't really make a profit, but...she won't mention that.

That's just Aria's kindness at work.

"Good morning, Vulcan!"

"Hey now—Aria, Tama, and Stella—good meowning!"

Before heading to the guild, Aria and company stop at Vulcan's Outfitters.

By the way—Aria did end up going back to her room at the inn to change her panties.

But let's forget that for now.

Vulcan's Outfitters is located quite close to the guild, and the party planned on meeting up with Vulcan before heading there.

Vulcan is completely prepared. She's wearing overalls with nothing underneath, as usual, but today she has on mithril alloy gauntlets and leggings, along with her trusty battle hammer, of course.

"Hey, Aria. I know you just got here, but can I hold Tama?"

Watching Aria hold Tama, Vulcan reaches out to her with a "meowww…!" and asks for a turn. Her side boob bounces up and down, looking velvety soft, when she stretches. Her gorgeous, tanned underarm is fully on display at the same time. Any gentleman with a thing for dark-skinned girls would be drooling.

"Of course you can! Tama, let's have Vulcan hold you, okay?"

"Meown—!"

Tama answers Aria directly. Obeying their master's orders is a knight's duty. Tama willingly accepts being passed to Vulcan.

"Meow—! Tama's fur is perfect, as usual—so fluffy and with a great sheen. It feels amazing!"

As she holds him, Vulcan thoroughly enjoys how good Tama feels in her arms, and she admires his fur.

There's no greater comfort than cuddling a fastidious creature like Tama.

Meown—I'm so jealous that Aria gets to live with this adorable and strong male feline! When Tama gets bigger, I wonder if he'll meow all night with her…?

Vulcan pictures the scene in her mind.

Quite a few beings in this world choose to intermingle with different races. As a member of the tiger-eared species, Vulcan herself is of mixed animal blood.

If she finds a strong, attractive male, it doesn't necessarily need to be a human. Above all else, Tama has saved Vulcan's life in the past. Because she doesn't have any issues with interspecies relations, that alone is enough for her to fall in love with Tama.

…? It looks like Vulcan is staring at Tama with tears in her eyes…

Aria realizes her friend looks a bit off but doesn't think to consider that she has fallen in love with Tama.

"Grrr… You are keeping him all to yourself…! Not fair!"

Stella grinds her teeth again—she can't count how many times she has today.

"Hey now, if it isn't Aria and party. Morning!"

"Good morning, Anna."

"Good meowning—!"

"Meown—!"

Arnold greets the party the second they step inside the guild. Aria, Vulcan, and Tama all reply enthusiastically.

Stella is watching carefully for a chance to pounce on Tama to hold him, but she's staring directly at him, and Aria knows what she's up to.

"Could you possibly be here for another quest, even though you're going on a long-distance assignment tomorrow?"

"You're correct, Anna. Do you have a quest that's light and easy?"

"Hmm, let's see... In that case, how does this sound?"

Arnold takes a single quest card out from underneath the reception counter.

"Um, this is... Urgh...ropers...?"

"Yes, we had a request to collect roper tentacles. Apparently, there is demand for them from doctors in the city. They gave a deadline of this evening, but the pay is quite exceptional. ♪"

The quest card Arnold presents is indeed for the delivery of roper tentacles. It may seem odd, but ropers' mucus and tentacles are used in a number of different medicines. It's likely the doctor requesting the raw materials has received a refinement request requiring them.

Just yesterday, Aria had a hell of a time at the hands of ropers thanks to Stella running off on her own in the labyrinth. Recalling what happened, the elf releases an audible groan.

"The pay is definitely good, meow. What do you think, Aria? We can have Stella go berserk until the ropers appear on the third level, and when we get there, you and I can clean them up, don'tcha think?"

"I see—that should allow us to finish up without falling into a similar situation as yesterday..."

Aria isn't super on board with Vulcan's suggestion, but she nods anyway. It's true there aren't that many short, simple quests that pay well. Plus, because ropers always move unpredictably, this is a good opportunity to train and keep her senses sharp.

Above all else, someone must be struggling if they put out a request like this. Aria's heightened sense of righteousness will not allow her to simply ignore it.

"That's correct, Stella. We'll be counting on you to take care of the enemies on the first and second levels, okay?"

"I hate when Aria bosses me around, but if I can go all out, then no problem. Also, I hate ropers, too!"

After yesterday, Stella has developed a considerable contempt for the creatures. She has no objections to the way today's quest is set to proceed.

Shrrrring—!

A sharp sound pierces the first level of the labyrinth—it's Stella's greatsword ripping through the air.

It mows down her goblin foes or squashes them flat as a pancake. For enemies on the first level, Stella doesn't require activating her dragonewt form, much less relying on her Mega Shield.

"Mm, Stella's very strong. But despite that..."

"It's a waste, meow. If she could just cooperate, she'd be the most powerful combination of attacker and tank, meow..."

Aria and Vulcan are once again blown away by Stella's over-the-top fighting style.

If only they had the same power and abilities...

If only she didn't have such a problematic personality...

She would be the most incredible talent.

It would be great if we could come up with a plan to encourage Stella to work with us when she fights, for the sake of tomorrow's quest...

Aria hasn't given up yet. She plans to get Stella to understand the importance of fighting side by side, no matter what. It's a critical step to keep her in this group, and if Stella ever decides to venture out on her own in the future, she'll probably end up joining another party. If by that point she still isn't able to coordinate with others in battle, she'll end up alienated. Aria, as her caretaker, is flush with a feeling of responsibility to make sure that never happens.

"Well, for meow the path forward has been cleared. Let's hustle and head to the next level right meow!"

They have complaints about Stella, but this is a time-sensitive quest. Vulcan gathers her wits about her and steps forward to lead them down to the next level.

The second level of the labyrinth—

"Bu-whooooooo—!"

As the party enters the next level, an orc—the most common monster inhabiting this area—screams and rushes toward them. It's holding its trademark club and appears to be very excited.

Really, that's a given—Aria's crew includes three absolutely bodacious babes, after all. Aria is in her bikini armor, Vulcan is naked underneath her overalls, and Stella is wearing low-rise hot pants and a jacket that shows her midriff, her cleavage, and her under boob...

Seeing the three girls dressed this way, the orc—a species known for its rampant lust—will naturally react accordingly.

As proof, the thing hanging between the orc's thighs is pointed directly upward, "ready to battle."

"Stella, right now, you don't need to worry about coordinating with us like yesterday—just go in for the kill, okay meow?!"

"You didn't have to even tell me!"

Answering Vulcan, Stella charges forward. She's taking this enemy a bit seriously, it would seem—she transforms into her dragonewt form as she goes to attack. Her arms grow several sizes larger, and a huge, rugged tail sprouts from the ass that was just peeking out from her shorts.

"This time, I'll practice my shield while I torment this pathetic soul!"

Stella's expression turns sadistic. She's feeling a bit stressed from not being able to rampage as hard as she wanted to yesterday. Granted, some of it comes from not being allowed to hold Tama, among other things...

Long story short, she's about to take it all out on this orc.

Ka-shinnn—

Stella's Mega Shield collides with the orc's club, sending sparks flying from the powerful impact.

—Stella, perfect timing. I'll show you how to use your shield.

—Tama! You know how to use one?!

Just as Stella goes on the defense, Tama shoots a telepathic message her way. In his past life, Tama was highly skilled with a shield. He means to teach her a few techniques, albeit verbally.

Even if they can't work directly in tandem, Tama has decided to at least show her some moves.

—First, push forward forcefully, then swipe your shield to the side!

—Okay!

Stella does as Tama instructs.

The next moment, the orc's club is brushed away, and the monster loses its balance.

—Incredible! With such little power, you broke the orc's stance!

—Hmm. It was pretty good for my first time. Okay, what's next...?

Following Tama's direction, Stella waits for the orc to stand up again, without going in for the kill. When it gets to its feet, Tama schools Stella in a number of new techniques to block its attacks.

It's unlikely she'll be able to master them all in a single day, but if she keeps practicing in the battles to come, she'll get the hang of it.

"H-huh… It looks like Stella's shield technique is improving—and quickly…"

"Aria, you think so, too, huh meow? It's almost like she's following someone's instructions, don'tcha think?"

She's a bit awkward, but Stella is deflecting her enemy's attacks. Aria and Vulcan are impressed.

Is Stella looking at Tama from time to time? It sure seems like he's staring back at her… Ha, there's no way.

Ensconced between Aria's breasts, Tama is staring at Stella and nodding each time she deflects an attack. Aria wonders, *Could Tama be giving her commands…?* but ends up laughing to herself, realizing how ridiculous that is.

Squelch, squelch, squee…!

A while after Stella's rampage—or rather, her shield training—finishes up, the party has arrived on the third level of the labyrinth. They immediately encounter a roper, the target of their quest.

"Aria, this time, we need to cut the tentacles off at their base and bring them home, okay meow?!"

"I am well aware, Vulcan. Tama, this is also training for me. You don't need to intervene unless it gets dangerous!"

"Meown—!" *Understood, master!*

Just as Vulcan says, the roper tentacles have to be severed at the base to fulfill their quest—thirty in total.

Ropers have six tentacles each, but cutting them off from the main body is no small task. Not to mention, the creatures will use their tentacles to attack Aria and company and try to impregnate them.

As Aria indicated, though, this is a chance for her to train and keep her senses sharp. Until she's unable to handle them all herself, she doesn't need Tama's help.

"Grrrr—!"

Stella is growling. Ropers are the natural enemies of all females.

Even though she realizes she won't be fighting right away this time, her natural instincts are setting off alarm bells.

—*Don't worry, Stella. I told you yesterday, but I am here to protect you. Just remain calm and watch my master fight.*

—*Tama! That's right! You will protect me, so I have nothing to be afraid of!!*

Stella couldn't be more pleased by Tama's reassurance.

Hmm. It seems like she's calmed down, but her shoulders are still tense. Nothing I can do…

Stella has stopped growling, but she's still gripping her weapon tightly. At this rate, any little thing could send her flying into a rampage.

If that happens, this encounter will be yesterday all over again. However, the party has entered the labyrinth with a quest today. They cannot leave without collecting the materials they came for.

To that end, Tama decides to ease Stella's stress even further. He trots over to where she stands…and suddenly jumps up lithely and lands on her right shoulder.

—*T-Tama! You willingly touched me!*

—*I'm here by your side. Just relax your shoulders.*

—*O-okay, got it!*

Being held by Stella…is still pretty terrifying, but Tama decides this is okay for now as he jumps up.

"Ngh… Tama's practically clinging to Stella… She's not exactly holding him, but…"

"Meow-ha-ha! Aria, you're jealous right meow, aren't you?!"

Aria also realizes that Tama has jumped on Stella's shoulder to soothe her. Even though she knows this, she sees Tama as a man, so for him to be touching her at all is enough to make her jealous.

Vulcan is amused by Aria's jealous sulking. It's so rare to see the elf envious that Vulcan can't help but erupt in laughter.

"Ugh, don't tell me you find this funny, Vulcan! …No matter. I'll take my anger out on the ropers."

Aria leaps toward the monsters, her cheeks still puffed out.

"Meown… I might have teased her a bit too much…"

Vulcan sheepishly follows Aria, and just then—

Sllllsppp—!

—each of the ropers shoots a single tentacle with incredible speed toward the two girls. These are much faster than the ones they faced yesterday. They must be older ropers that know the…ropes.

Aria can tell they're higher level.

"Acceleration—!"

Aria cries out and activates her innate skill, Acceleration, reaching top speed in an instant. She dodges the high-speed tentacles with ease and rushes up to the monsters.

"It's no use, slimeballs—!"

Vulcan is already on the move. She sticks her battle hammer out in front of her and skillfully wraps the tentacles around it. Just like that, she pulls with all her might and rips the tentacles from their stem—*rrrpppplllsh—!*

"Pi-gyaaaaaaaa—!"

What an epic maneuver! The roper screams in agony from the searing pain, and its movements become more sluggish.

This is the perfect opportunity—Aria swings her knives at the roper. Her aim is sure as she cuts off three tentacles on its right side in one slash. She turns to slice off the other three on its left but runs into trouble.

The roper withstands the searing pain and reaches out to attack Aria with its three remaining appendages... However—

"No chance meow—!"

Vulcan whirls around to the monster's left side without her battle hammer in hand.

"Enchant Ice!"

Vulcan activates her derived skill Enchant Ice, and a layer of subzero-degree ice forms around her gauntlets.

Gah-shhhhhh—!

Vulcan grabs all the tentacles with both hands, and they freeze solid. It doesn't quite manage to freeze the roper's main body, but it's definitely enough to stop the tentacles from moving.

"Aria, do it meow—!"

"You got it, Vulcan!"

With its tentacles paralyzed, the roper is helpless. It tries to escape but doesn't have a chance. Vulcan pulls on the monster's tentacles, immobilizing it.

Aria proceeds to use her knives to rip through the remaining tentacles with an audible slash.

"Your time's up! Enchant Flame!"

To finish the roper off, Vulcan activates her derived skill Enchant Flame. Her hand becomes a flaming blade and pierces the creature directly in its heart.

"*Pi-gyaaaaaaaa—!*"

The roper's death knell echoes through the labyrinth. In a final show of resistance, mucus audibly sprays from the stubs of its amputated tentacles.

"Eeeeek—!"

"Oh meowwww! It got us!"

Sticky white mucus explodes all over Aria's and Vulcan's faces.

Both girls are sweaty from battle, their cheeks flushed scarlet, and their breath comes out in ragged gasps.

They certainly look like they've been finished off...

M-master, it pains me to see you in such a state...!

Tama stares at Aria despondently from atop Stella's shoulder.

"Well, hey now—welcome back! ♪"

Arnold greets Aria and company as they return that afternoon to the guild from the labyrinth. He sees the tentacles sticking out of Aria's backpack and is relived that they've successful completed their quest.

As the guild receptionist, the moments Arnold feels the greatest joy are when he sees adventurers returning safe and sound from a mission. In particular, Aria is someone he's cared for like his own daughter. Every time she comes back from a quest, Arnold breathes a sigh of relief.

"Hi, Anna! We're back!"

"Meown—today's quest went really well, didn't it meow?"

Aria and Vulcan took down close to ten ropers today, and the satisfaction is apparent in their grins. They both got a thorough workout, and their faces are flushed red, their skin covered in a light sweat.

Enveloped in Aria's breasts is Tama, who's out cold from the pheromones being secreted with her sweat, lazing away tucked in her soft bosom.

"Hey now—Stella, you sure look like you're in a good mood!"

In response, Stella chuckles, "Heh-heh-heh...! Tama jumped up on my shoulder by himself today! This is a step in the right direction!"

Stella looks thoroughly pleased with herself.

Judging from her disposition the day before, Arnold thought she would point out Aria's weaknesses or complain she didn't get to rampage enough, but the day's happy circumstances enable her to forget these things.

"That sounds like great news, Stella! ♪"

Arnold smiles happily at the young woman, who responds with the same self-satisfied expression.

"Okay then, I'll begin appraising your items, so go ahead and relax while you wait, all right?"

"Understood, Anna!"

"Hey, let's all get a drink at the bar, meow! We need to give you a boost for your quest tomorrow, Aria!"

"Oh, great idea! Let's do it!"

At Vulcan's suggestion, Aria and her companions proceed to the bar for a tipple while they wait for their materials to be assessed. It might be a bit early for a drink, but they'll be departing tomorrow at the crack of dawn.

In that case, they'll nourish themselves with some delicious food and a bit of drink before settling in for the night.

"Okay, Stella, it's time to get some food."

"What?! Oh my god, I can't believe I haven't eaten yet! I want some meat!"

"Hee-hee, Stella, you really love meat, don't you?"

Aria and company head to the guild bar while conversing. They place an order with the bar maid… That is, they basically order a massive amount of meat. It's clear to them that Stella won't be satisfied with a small portion. She also eats really quickly, so they go ahead and order extra from the start.

"Okay! I hereby propose a toast to Aria and her party's success on their long-distance quest tomorrow! Cheers meow!"

"Cheers!"

At Vulcan's toast, Aria raises her glass filled with honey liqueur.

Stella doesn't understand what a toast is but exclaims, "Huh, seems fun!" and holds up her glass.

Tama mews loudly in front of the saucer of milk he's been provided.

"Sorry to keep you waiting!"

Shortly after their toast, just as Stella starts fidgeting nervously in expectation of her meal, a number of dishes arrive at their table.

"Wh-what is this, this smell...?! It's making me unspeakably hungry!"

"Stella, this is called steak. This kind in particular is a regional specialty flavored with salt, pepper, and a special sauce, and... Wait, are you even listening...?"

Aria tries to explain the dish to her, but Stella is clearly overcome by the incredible aroma. She's gazing at the plate in front of her with drool dangling from her mouth.

"Stella, let's dig right in!"

Just as Stella exclaims, "Yeah! I'm gonna eat so much—!" her hand stops. She's looking back and forth between the steak stuck on her fork and Tama.

Both Aria and Vulcan stare at Stella blankly, completely perplexed.

"T-Tama, thank you for making me happy today!"

Incredibly, Stella manages to show the little behemoth some gratitude. She looks beyond embarrassed as her cheeks flush red. She then takes her fork with steak stuck on it and pushes it toward Tama.

Her hand is shaking ever so slightly. Previously, when she asked Tama to open wide, he turned away from her. She is terrified that the same thing will happen today.

—*What? I told you that I would protect you. That much is a given. And today, you didn't even run off on your own. That's admirable.*

Tama communicates telepathically with Stella as she stares at him, her eyes wavering, and he chomps down on the bite-size piece of steak.

Tama praised me! And he opened wide to eat my food!

Stella's expression brightens. This is her first time being complimented by Tama. That alone would raise her spirits, but she also succeeded in getting him to allow her to feed him, which he refused just yesterday.

She is so elated that her eyes begin welling up.

"Hmph… Tama cheated on me…"

"Meown, Aria, you're more the jealous type than I thought…"

Seeing Tama and Stella gaze into each other's eyes, Aria puffs up her cheeks and sulks yet again.

Hmm? Master, you seem upset…

Tama is sensitive and realizes something isn't quite right with Aria, but he's unable to read her innermost thoughts.

"Bath time, it's bath time—!"

Aria looks positively joyful as she strides down the stairs with Tama in tow.

A while after finishing dinner—

Aria and company returned to the inn and decided to head down for a bath. Vulcan is with them today; anyone can use the inn's bath for a fee.

"The bubbles in the bath get all foamy and pop! So fun!"

Stella is gleefully following Aria down the stairs. After her first bathing experience the other day, she's already a huge fan. Stella's really looking forward to bath time as she swings the towel Aria bought her.

"Meown—I haven't been in the bath with Tama for a long time; I can hardly wait!"

Vulcan has brought a towel and change of clothes from home, and she can't wait to bathe with cute little Tama.

"Th-these three babes are…"

"Gonna take…a bath together…?!"

The girls can hear men who look like adventurers whispering to one another from the lobby. They're creeping behind the girls to see if they can catch a glimpse of them in the bath—or at the very least, a glimpse of them changing.

However, they're quickly stopped in their tracks by the proprietress's fists.

Whoooosh—!

In the changing room, Stella instantly sheds her jacket. She doesn't look embarrassed in the slightest as she rips it off excitedly. The second she does, her bountiful bosom jiggles and ripples with splendor. In the next moment, she's out of her tiny hot pants, too.

She removes her panties in the same swift motion, putting her privates and their lovely hues directly in Tama's line of sight. He rushes to avert his gaze.

Next to Stella, Vulcan is taking off her overalls. She doesn't wear a bra, and her delectable twin peaks—which are always visible under her overalls—are now fully exposed.

Her back and stomach are both a healthy shade of golden wheat, while the small mounds at the center of each peak are nicely pink.

She's wearing tiger-striped shorts perfectly suited for a sprightly beast girl.

Beside Vulcan, Aria is also undressing. She carefully strips off her bikini armor, exposing her favorite tiny black bra and thong panties.

Her muscular yet plump figure boasts perfect proportions. Even when she removes her lingerie, her breasts and rear end don't budge. Nothing about her undergarments belies the figure beneath them.

"Meown—! Your breasts are so big, Aria! Stella and I have big boobs, too, but you're on a different level!"

"Grrr, is the reason Tama is always being held by Aria because she has the biggest boobs? Or because they're the softest? I must find out!"

"Eh? Wai— Stella, what are you...? Ahhh! Don't rub my breasts!"

"Shut up and sit still!"

As Vulcan admires the size of Aria's breasts, Stella starts massaging them out of curiosity. The elf tries to resist, but Stella overpowers her, pushing into her breasts forcefully, kneading and twisting her massive twin peaks like potter's clay.

"No fair meow! I'm joining in!"'

Vulcan gets carried away and joins the fray, sliding around Aria to knead her breasts from behind.

Ah-ahhh... No! Tama...Tama is watching! He's watching me getting groped!

It was meant only to be a little mischievous fun among girls... When Aria sees Tama looking at her worriedly, though, she becomes more stimulated than ever before. She pants seductively and begins rubbing her thighs together.

"Meown?! Aria, don't tell me you're..."

Seeing her sudden transformation, Vulcan realizes that her friend is getting aroused.

The girls have gone too far, and Vulcan starts to tell Stella, "Okay, that's enough meow." However...

"These breasts are unbelievably soft! I better find out how soft *these* are, too!"

...before Vulcan can stop her, Stella reaches for Aria's nipples—erect and perfectly light pink—and squeezes them between her index fingers and thumbs.

"—……—‼"

Aria squeals wordlessly, her knees knocking together from the spasms.

"Meownnn—?!" *Master?!*

Tama cries out in shock at the sudden turn of events.

"N-no… Tama, dun lookit meee… ♡"

Tama approaches Aria in a panic, but she barely manages to say "don't look" in a sultry voice. Her breath is ragged, and her cheeks are flushed. Tiny pink hearts float in her gorgeous ice-blue eyes.

"Wh-what's going on?!"

"Meownnn—?! Now we've really done it…!"

Aria crumples to the floor, knock-kneed. Between her erratic breathing and the look on her face, she has completely and utterly surrendered to her most carnal emotions.

Stella looks absolutely perplexed by the spectacle, while Vulcan, who knows exactly what's happening, puts her head in her hands and moans, "What have we done?!"

She can't believe a little girl-on-girl prank would do *this* to Aria…

Vulcan can't help but feel responsible for going overboard.

⚜

"Ughhh… That was awful. And they did it in front of my beloved, of all people…"

Twenty or so minutes later, Aria has managed to recover and curses her companions under her breath as she soaks in the bath.

"W-we're so sorry, meow! We had no idea *that* would happen, really we didn't…"

"Urgh… I don't get it, but I am sorry…"

Vulcan apologizes to Aria, looking positively remorseful. Stella is soaking in the bath next to them and offers her own teary-eyed apology. She has a huge bump on her head—Vulcan rapped her with her knuckles for escalating the situation too far.

Stella didn't expect Vulcan to get mad at her and is shocked. She wasn't told exactly why it was wrong but understands she did a bad thing and is remorseful.

"Meown—!" *Master, are you okay...?*

Tama mews worriedly at Aria while floating in the bath. He hasn't realized what actually happened to Aria.

He's concerned she's sick.

"Hee-hee... Tama, you are such a sweetheart. ♡ Come over here, okay?"

Aria squeezes Tama tightly from behind, and the soft sensation causes a mew replete with relief to escape him.

"Grrr—! Not fair! I want to clutch Tama to my bosom, too!"

"Meown—! Tama's face looks so cute when he's tucked between your boobs, like he's at complete peace."

Stella puts her index finger to her lips and stares enviously at Tama.

Vulcan, meanwhile, is crushing hard on Tama's adorable little face.

Tama, someday...when you get bigger, let's meow *together all night, okay?* ♡

Aria grins from ear to ear as she stares at Tama, sleepily floating in the tub, and imagines what possibilities the future might hold...

It's been quite a long time—it's me, the author Nozomi Ginyoku. Thank you for purchasing the second volume of this novel. How did you like Volume 2 of *I'm a Behemoth, an S-Ranked Monster, but Mistaken for a Cat, I Live as an Elf Girl's Pet*?

The side story at the end of this volume was pretty over-the-top—I hope you enjoyed it.

The manga adaptation is also now on sale, and there's a promotion going on where you'll receive a free gift with the purchase of both this book and the manga. Please see the cover ad for details.

Also, there's a companion novel to *I'm a Behemoth* that takes place in the same universe. It's called *Onna Yuusha ni Jibun no Seidorei ni Naranai to Paatei wo Tsuihou Suru to Odosareta no de Ridatsu wo Sentaku Shimasu (The Heroine Threatened to Kick Me Out of the Party if I Didn't Become Her Sex Slave, So I Decided to Defect)* and is scheduled for release on October 25. If you like *I'm a Behemoth*, I'm sure you'll enjoy this series as well, so please take a moment to check it out.

That's all I have to say for now.

I look forward to seeing you again in any of my other works or once Volume 3 (hopefully!) comes out!

Nozomi Ginyoku

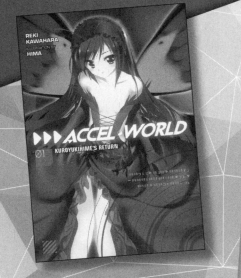

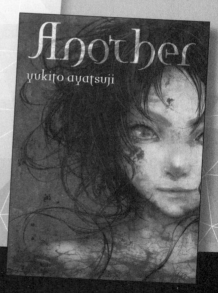